BONE DANCE

Also by the author
Traveling On into the Light and Other Stories

BONE DANCE

Martha Brooks

Orchard Books New York

Orchard Books, 95 Madison Avenue, New York, NY 10016

Manufactured in the United States of America
Book design by Mina Greenstein
The text of this book is set in 11.5 Sabon
10 9 8 7 6 5 4 3 2 1

Library of Congress Cataloging-in-Publication Data
Brooks, Martha, date.
Bone dance / by Martha Brooks.
p. cm.
Summary: When her father wills her a cabin on land in
rural Manitoba, Alexandra meets a young man who
shares her Native Canadian heritage and her experience of
being guided by spirits.
ISBN 0-531-30021-8.—ISBN 0-531-33021-4 (lib. bdg.)
[1. Parent and child—Fiction. 2. Spirituality—Fiction.
3. Dreams—Fiction. 4. Indians of North America—
Canada—Fiction. 5. Canada—Fiction.] I. Title.
PZ7.B7975Bo 1997 [Fic]—dc21 97-10230

106361

For my daughter,
Kirsten Jay Brooks, Blue Wolf

———————

And the memory of her beloved grandfather,
Alfred Leroy Paine

"Humankind has not woven the web of life. We are but one thread within it. Whatever we do to the web we do to ourselves. All things are bound together. All things connect. Whatever befalls the Earth befalls the children of the Earth."

—CHIEF SEATTLE,
from his address to the president of the
United States, 1855

———————

"In the purity of the morning, I see how much more there is to the world than meets the eye. . . ."

—SHARON BUTALA,
from *The Perfection of the Morning:*
An Apprenticeship in Nature

part one

THE SPIRITS

1

*I*n the middle of the night, in the middle of her eleventh-grade year, in the middle of the coldest Manitoba winter for a century, Grandpa called to say that he was worried about "the dark."

"It's night, Grandpa. It's night and time to go to bed."

"It just rolls in, Alex," he continued, "and all I can do is watch. It's terrible. I can't sleep."

She knew that the cancer wouldn't let him sleep. Plus, lately he seemed confused. A nurse was with him during the day. Then Alex and Mom and Auntie Francine took turns being with him during the evening. At midnight, when they were back in their own beds, it was hard to turn off thoughts, to sleep, peacefully to dream.

"I'll come over. Okay?" Tears tumbled down her cheeks onto her red turtleneck sweater, which she hadn't bothered to change out of before falling into bed. "I'll be right there, Grandpa."

"No," he said, clearing his throat, reclaiming his

dignity. "No, Alexandra Marie Sinclair. You need to rest. I shouldn't have called. I just wanted to hear your voice one more time today. How's school?"

She didn't want him to die. But how could she wish for her grandpa to stay with all that he had suffered?

"Grandpa," she said, "I love you. Please try to go to sleep. You need to rest, too."

"Well, I've worried you. This isn't like me," he said forlornly, reading her mind as usual. "I'm not myself lately."

She got off the phone and rolled back into bed but couldn't sleep. She kept seeing him up in his apartment, slack-jawed, watching in terror as the dark pressed against his fourteenth-floor living-room window. She thought about the mysteries of the universe and about how, soon, they would all unfold for him. And about how she'd be left behind. And about how this was becoming a pattern in her life.

When her mother was nineteen years old, she came home late one night, marched into the kitchen, and announced to Grandpa and Grandma, who was then still alive, "I'm going to marry Earl McKay. And there isn't a damn thing you can do about it."

Well, they didn't stop her. And it became an infamous family story. "She was the most unstoppable young woman," Grandpa said. "Stubborn. Full of pride. Of course we worried that it would end up bad. And we were right. Earl McKay didn't choose to stick around after you were born. But it did mean that I got to spend more time with you. So there you go!

Life is full of surprises, and sometimes the good ones and the bad ones get all bunched up together."

According to Auntie Francine, Alex was badly spoiled by them all. "If you asked for the moon," said Francine, "Grandpa Paul would hang it shining around your neck in a minute. But we've all spoiled you. We're to blame for lavishing all this love on you so that you've come to expect it, like royalty."

"Don't be ridiculous, Auntie."

"It's true," said Francine, grabbing her close, kissing her hair. "You've always been marked for something special. Just don't let it go to your head."

Three nights after Grandpa called about the dark, Alex was out with Serena Fitzpatrick and Andrea Larkin and Jeremy Huntinghawk in the snowy park down the street. It was the only place nearby where she could find the solace of the country in the middle of the city. On this prairie winter night, deep in the sleeping heart of January, it was twenty-six below zero. The only light was the moon, dazzling down on the snow.

They played tag all through the cathedral of frozen trees. And then Jeremy said, "Okay, now, on the count of three, everybody howl."

They threw back their heads and counted, and then they howled. Like feral creatures. Like heartsick lonely wolves. And it felt so good as they ran through the snow crying, "A-wooo!" at the flying moon. "A-wah-wah-woooo!"

She stopped to watch the others howling and

leaping. And it was at this moment that she knew her grandfather had just moved, without saying good-bye, far beyond her reach. With absolute certainty, her heart thudding against her chest, she knew that he had slipped past her, past them all, past the dark of winter and midnight and consciousness and eating and sleeping and caring. Then she watched as her own breath rose in front of her astonished eyes, took form, and floated like a spirit hand on the crystal air.

2

The end of a hot dusty day in early August. Lonny pulled the truck off the road. The wheels bumped down the rutted grassy trail. Leaf-rattling poplar trees crowded in, then chokecherry bushes, scraping past the windows, thrumming the silver aerial.

The trail ended in the wide clearing that overlooked Fatback Lake. They lurched to a halt. Earl McKay slowly got down from the passenger's side, blinking his eyes like a newborn baby.

Lonny got out, too, shoving his hands in the pockets of his jeans, showing this worn-out cowboy that he was more casual than he felt. Showing him this property that had been in his stepfather's family since the first LaFrenière, a Métis trapper and buffalo hunter, took up land along the lake and up into the Lacs des Placottes Valley hills.

The ancestral LaFrenière log cabin, once snug and sturdy, was as gray and sagging as an abandoned wasp's nest. Behind that were the cut banks, the hills, and that particular one with its Indian burial mound that everyone for miles around called Medicine Bluff. As always, the mound was rosy and beautiful in the fading light of day. As always, he could feel the presence of the furious spirits rising around it.

"I'll haul in that old house trailer your stepdad offered me," said Earl. "Then I'll build my own little place where I can sit high and dry and watch the lake break up next spring, yessir." He lined his finger up to the woodlands—the white birches, the scrub oaks, the poplars, the rocks where mosses grew, the sloping banks—and slowly turned three hundred and sixty degrees until he faced the lake again.

"I've got to admit," he continued with a satisfied sigh, "this place is as close to heaven as I'm ever going to find. I'm half a century old and tired of moving around."

He looked sharply at Lonny. "What made your stepdad change his mind and decide to sell?"

Lonny kicked at the tires. "It's not good for anything," he mumbled.

"Now I know you're being modest. You were raised right close. Isn't that true?"

"Since I was seven," Lonny said, and then wished he hadn't.

"*Seven?* Why, that's most of your lifetime, boy. Isn't that so? Don't *you* want to keep it?"

None of your damn business, he thought, his jaw muscles tightening.

Earl persisted. "Figured the way your stepdad feels about you, that'd be the last thing he'd want to sell. Land that's been in the family for generations."

In the neighboring farms, everyone knew enough to avoid talking about the selling of this particular parcel of land. There was Jacob Wiebe, for instance. Out of respect and affection for Pop, he talked around it, standing beside his truck, saying things like, "Well, Tom, one thing's for sure, time don't stand still." Avoiding Pop's eyes. Squinting instead at the sun. "If you need anything, don't you hesitate to ask."

But Earl McKay didn't seem to have any sense of what Pop called good old-fashioned country propriety.

"I don't want to rush you," said Lonny, "but I have to get back pretty soon."

He couldn't wait to get back into the truck and take the hell off. Away from the whisperings of the Ancients. Away to the safety of the prairie farm road.

Earl McKay was in no hurry. He sniffed the air as if he were a man just let out of prison. As if he truly didn't understand that some places had the power to do anything they wanted to you. Well, let him find out for himself. There was nothing in the world that was going to stop him now. He'd been back twice already, making the trip on the bus from Lethbridge across two provinces with one eye, probably, on the horizon, just counting the minutes until he owned the LaFrenière homestead.

Back at home Pop had served them all the last of the venison soup from the deer he'd shot early this spring and cut up and put in their freezer.

It had only been half-grown. "We have to eat, son," was all the explanation Pop had given Lonny the day he'd come dragging it home through the bush. Lonny had just gotten off the school bus. He'd stood in the yard with a *History of the Modern World* textbook and two ridiculously bright purple binders tucked under his arm. He pushed his glasses back up his nose and stared hard at the deer. Its head wobbled back in the snow. A thin string of blood and mucus came from its nose.

Since then, things had been gradually improving. Pop had sold everything but the homestead and another small piece of land: five acres of hills and woodlands and pasture where they still lived in the bright yellow bungalow. He'd found work at the Beaver Lumber store in town. In a few short months, he'd worked himself up to assistant manager, and he went about this job with a quiet dignity even though his heart wasn't in it. His heart was still on the land, and Lonny knew it probably always would be.

Lonny also had found work. Part-time at a gas station that didn't mind that his hair curved down past his shoulders. Mr. Johnson, his boss, had told Pop, "That big boy of yours is real personable. A charmer, just like his mother was. Everybody likes Lonny."

Everybody except those damn spirits. At least, since he was twelve years old, they'd stopped coming into his bedroom at night.

3

Robert Lang, his oldest friend in the world, poked his head in the truck window, leaned on one arm, nodded his head after the retreating Earl McKay, and said, "So who's the cowboy?"

"Buying up the homestead," said Lonny, watching Earl's back disappear into the house. "He's gone inside with Pop."

"And how's he taking it?" Robert pulled back, looked down at his feet, kicked lightly at the side of the truck.

"Not good."

"You going into town later?"

"I don't know," said Lonny. "Maybe. Why?"

"A party. Over at Sherry-Lynne Baker's place. I came all this way to tell you about it, stud," he drawled.

"Yeah, all five miles." Lonny grinned at goofy Robert.

"So," said Robert cheerfully, "you gonna join us? Or you gonna stay home and baby-sit your pop?"

"Don't know," said Lonny, resenting that last remark.

"Come on," Robert urged. "What's he going to do once you move out? Things'll just keep goin' on the same old way as they have since your ma died. Whether you're there or not. Nothing you can do to change that. Am I right?"

"That's not the point. He shouldn't be alone tonight."

"Suit yourself." Robert drummed a happy little beat on the truck door. "Don't drag your ass out on my account."

"I'll think about it, man." Lonny flopped his head back on the seat and wondered how much more of this he could take. I owe that man in there my life, he thought, and all I ever seem to do is watch him suffer again and again. What a pathetic world.

Robert, reaching in, lightly punched Lonny's shoulder. "It isn't your fault that he's selling. Cut yourself a little slack there, buddy. It's his decision, right?" And then he left.

His decision. A savings account earmarked for other things, special things, Pop said. What special things? Well, for your life. Imagine, you could be the first LaFrenière to get a real education.

God knows he didn't want the homestead, and Pop understood this. He didn't have to say a single word. The property, and all that it had meant to over one hundred years of LaFrenières, was itself a ghost. It hovered between them, anxious, alert to the currents of human emotion.

Well, maybe now, Lonny thought, he'll start to forget. And then, God help me, I can, too.

But it wasn't going to be easy. Several hours later Pop stood in the kitchen like a man lost in his own house. And then, when Lonny couldn't think of what else to do, he asked if he could get him anything.

"No, no." Pop shook his head, slowly leaned over. Picked up a button that, hanging by a thread, had finally toppled off his sweater onto the floor. Turned it over thoughtfully. Looked at it. Put it in his pocket. He wiped his hand over his face, looked up at the moon that had risen outside the kitchen window. "It's been a long day," he said.

Lonny thought about another day. The deep blue sky of autumn. The truck ride, with his new stepfather, onto the property. Mr. LaFrenière smiled his big gap-toothed smile, took his cap, put it on Lonny.

He was small back then, even for seven. When they got out of the truck, Pop called him a sack of potatoes. He picked him up and threw him over his shoulder and carried him, yelling for the cap that had just flown off. Lonny laughed, upside down. The ground was the sky and the sky, the ground.

"And now, I'm going to show you the prettiest sight in all of Manitoba," Pop said, sliding Lonny down off his back.

Lonny rushed back to get the cap, then roared after him, through the bushes, pumping his small sturdy legs to keep up with Pop, who was climbing up Medicine Bluff just like he had no legs at all. Like he had wings for feet.

At the top, both of them out of breath, Pop sat down, pulling Lonny beside him. He reached to smooth a silvery green plant with his hand. "Smell," he said, and Lonny bent over and inhaled for the first time the pungent medicinal smell of prairie sage.

A September sun shone fully on the straw-colored grasses. A flock of pelicans flew over the lake below, gliding like thunderheads just above the surface of the water.

But what Lonny remembered noticing most of all was the silence. And the peaceful feeling that grew right up inside him. This big prairie country was filled for miles around with the sounds of wind and crickets. A car crawled silently along the yellow gravel road at the other side of the valley.

"This, that we are sitting on," Pop had said, indicating the slight contour that rose a couple of feet above the natural top of the hill. "This is an Indian burial mound. It has the distinction of being one of the few left in this province that hasn't been dug up and inspected by grave robbers."

"Robbers?"

"My grandfather—and that would be your great-grandfather by association, since you have now become a LaFrenière—he broke his back buffalo hunting. Can you imagine a time that long ago?"

"Did he get better?"

"Oh, yes. But this land that you see all around, it was here before him. It was here before the earliest people. And most certainly it was here before the French and the English. *And* the Métis," he said, indi-

cating his own heart. "It's old, Lonny. Old as time.
So that's why we have to take care of it. It's our job.
Our responsibility." He paused, patted the mound.
"Here rest the bones of an ancient person."

"Here? Right here?"

"That's right."

"How do you know he's ancient?" Lonny liked the
sound of the word.

"Because those first people, they buried their most
revered in the highest places. Right beneath us rest
the bones of a medicine man. Or maybe a great chief!
Or my name isn't Thomas LaFrenière." He paused
dramatically. Lonny leaned against him and looked
up into his face.

Pop chuckled, reached down, and tugged the cap
brim over Lonny's eyes. "Let's go home now," he
said, "and see that mother of yours. If we stay away
too long, we might make her mad at us men."

"So, my babe," she said when he and Pop scuffed
up the porch steps, knocking mud off their boots,
"how was that? Did you like it? Come here." She
pulled him onto her lap, tickling his ear.

"It was like that time I saw the light on the trees!"
he told her excitedly. "That's *just* how it felt!"

One day, back in the city, she'd told him that if you
settled down and were very quiet, you could see light
come right out and dance on the branches after the
long, hard winter. "Mmm-hmm, really, I wouldn't lie
to you. See that tree, now?" She pointed out past the
little south-facing window of their tiny apartment.
"Sit down and stare real hard at it."

He sat down on the floor with his hands in his lap, just like they did on *Sesame Street,* and then he stared hard at the tree. His eyes made big tears from concentration, and just when he was ready to give up, she said, "Keep looking," from the sofa where she sat folding socks and little shirts. He kept looking, to please her. And then the bare limbs of that spring tree *did* begin to shimmer with dancing light! With points and beads and ripples of pale gold that slowly bleached out and filled his eyes.

A year after she married Pop, his mom, glowing and big and beautiful, went into the hospital to give birth to his baby sister. She came home empty-armed and sad. The light went out around her. He was eight years old and had never before been to a funeral.

He crept into Pop's arms. It was a cold spring day. "It's okay, it's okay," Pop said over and over again. "We'll be all right. Things will be okay again."

And, after a while, they were. Wild, blond ex-hippie Deena came into their yard. She appeared, a month later, in June, on a chestnut red horse. She slipped off the animal's back, extended her tanned hand to Lonny's mom, and said, "I'm Deena. I live down the road. It's time we met."

"Deena." Pop, coming up from the barn, looked at her in stunned surprise. "Thought you ran off to Calgary."

She flushed, and Lonny thought she was beautiful. "Been back over a month," she said. "Couldn't stay in the city a minute longer. Got restless again. Discovered I couldn't breathe. So I guess this is going to be my home after all."

"That's good," said Pop, and a little current, like the flutter of invisible wings, flew between them, then vanished.

A big freckly grin now covered Deena's face. "Didn't you hear? My uncle died and left me a pile of money. I just bought the old café in town. And who might you be?" She tucked her strong, lemony, horsey-smelling fingers under Lonny's chin. Then she turned her eyes back to Lonny's mom. "I don't suppose there's a person in this community who hasn't heard about your loss. I hear a good eighty percent turned up for the funeral. That's some outpouring of love. But I sure am sorry for what you must be going through." Her boots were the same shiny color as her horse, who now arched its neck and nudged her shoulder.

Lonny's mom turned her face away. He and Pop stood looking at her, caught in their desperate hope for some happy response. In that instant he knew two things: that they both loved her beyond measure, and that their lives were spun together out of the silk of her very breath.

She turned back and, reaching out, took Deena's hand. She urged her shyly toward the house. "Come inside," she said. "I'll make us some tea."

His mom changed after that. She seemed a different person. She was more demanding, less willing to stick around the farm and just be with Lonny and Pop. But she wasn't crying anymore, and that was a big plus.

"Deena's coming over," she'd say. "We're all going into town now. She's wallpapering her restaurant today. Tom, where's that paste you've been holding on to? We don't need it anymore."

And at the grand opening of Deena's Deli, Deena made a big speech about finding friends in places where you'd hardly expect they'd be.

That night, the night of the opening, Lonny overheard Pop say softly to his mom, "Deena and I had a little something going. That was a long time ago. Before you came along and stole my heart."

His mom, in the shocking quiet of their kitchen, said, "I knew that."

"You knew? She told you?"

"She didn't have to. It took courage for her to come and be my friend."

And so, life went on like that for quite a while. A little sister never got to be part of their family. The plans that had been made around her arrival—the freshly painted wicker bassinet that had held generations of LaFrenière babies, the little blue room off Mom and Pop's bedroom, the talk of a family of four—were replaced by Deena, what she was doing, what she thought about this and that. She was included in family horseback rides in the summer and skating at the rink in town in the winter. And as Lonny grew and took the rural bus to school and started making friends of his own, he didn't think too much more about that heightened time, about the strange and sad and brave world of grown-ups.

* * *

A week after Earl McKay moved onto the old LaFrenière land, Lonny woke up in his room, his chest
heaving with tears. His sobs were so awful and uncon-
trollable, he was afraid he would wake up Pop.

He had been dreaming of his mother. She had
appeared to him as a vision in a shiny white dress
decorated with beads the color of the sunrise and long,
soft feathery fringe. She had never worn such a dress
when she was alive. She came and sat on his bed,
crossed her legs, thoughtfully jigged one foot up and
down. "Lonny, my babe," she said at last in a sad
and disappointed voice, "how come you did that? It's
a sacred place."

He wanted her to tell him that she loved him, to
turn and to cling to her, to keep her close inside his
heart. But she just put her hands on her knees and
shook her head. "You were supposed to take care of
it, not dig it up. Why couldn't you leave those poor
souls in peace?" And then she got up and left through
his bedroom door.

Robert Lang was the only person who shared his
guilty secret. And it had all started so innocently. A
badger kicked something out of its den on Medicine
Bluff.

It was the year he turned eleven. He and Robert, a
couple of raunchy kids, had gone up there, their packs
full of sandwiches and cookies and soft drinks and
some contraband magazines belonging to Robert's
older brother, Danny. It was a sizzling hot July after-

noon, and Medicine Bluff was their favorite place to be.

Near the top of the slope they saw something bony lying just outside the opening of the badger's den. Lonny reached down and rolled it over. Faceup. It was a small human skull. Its toothless jaws, its round vacant eyes, stared up at him. This was not the skull of a great chief or medicine man. It was not much bigger than his hand. So much for Pop's theory. He turned to say something to Robert, and he was gone, already at the bottom of the hill and still running. But twenty minutes later, back at home, Robert took the tiny skull out of Lonny's hands.

"Look!" he said, rolling it over to show Pop how the base of the skull had been crushed.

"Wasn't done in by badgers," Pop said, staring hard through his grease-speckled glasses. "Stone war mallet, probably."

He sat on an old stool in the shed, cleaning motor parts, wiping them down with a rag, his big bony hands covered with black grease.

"You told me a great chief was buried there, Pop," said Lonny, feeling cheated.

"Probably more than one person buried up there. We'll never know for sure." Pop looked straight into Lonny's eyes. "We have to leave them be, son."

A westerly breeze blew through the open door and windows, and Lonny's mom appeared, leaning against the doorway. "What's up?" Her cool slim fingers reached to tuck his hair behind his ears.

"Look what we found!" Robert turned proudly

with their prize still cupped in his hands. Her eyes widened.

"We found it on Medicine Bluff," Lonny told her. "A badger dug it up."

"Bury it," she said, turning away. "Go back there, and bury it."

"Can't we keep it awhile?" Lonny pleaded.

Pop bent again over his work. "Do what your mother says. Even badgers have no business disturbing the dead."

"He was just being a badger." Lonny pouted.

"Spade's over there in the corner," said Pop.

So he and Robert took the spade and the skull, reluctantly got on their bikes, and wheeled back to Medicine Bluff.

"Stupid badger," said Lonny, pressing his foot on the blade, digging deep into the rich dark heart of the hill. The smell of sage and bergamot rose up from the loamy upturned soil. The badger was either not at home or had moved somewhere else. Lonny kept on digging.

Robert stood beside him, arms folded. "Are you going to just keep doing that? How much more are you going to dig?"

"Shut up," said Lonny. "Don't ask dumb questions."

"I want to dig, too. I want to find out what's in there."

"Then take the damn shovel. Here."

They took turns digging. They unearthed what might have been the remains of a child: a leg bone, a small rib, a tiny skeletal hand. By then, neither of them was brave enough to stop. Only a couple of feet beneath the surface of the mound, they began to unearth a complete skeleton, a big one. It was buried in a crouching position. They dug with the shovel. They dug with their hands. They found a shell necklace, a portion of a clay pot, a perfect pale arrowhead mixed in with the bones of the skeleton's ribs. They dug with a queer and giddy energy until Lonny shot up from the mound and sat on the edge of it, grabbing mouthfuls of air.

He prayed for the sun to vaporize the feelings that were creeping in around him. Down the hill the poplar leaves shook like tongues in the wind.

Robert came up from the mound, too, gasping. His freckles stood out like startled dots against his white skin. "I feel sick," he said, weaving back down one side of the hill.

When Robert returned, Lonny quickly swiped tears from his eyes with the backs of his hands.

"I didn't think it'd be like this," Robert said.

"Liar," said Lonny. "What'd you think we'd find— a couple of arrowheads?"

"Why didn't you stop?"

"Why didn't *you* stop?"

They put everything back as best they could. They even patted back the clumps of prairie grass and flowers, the blazing star, the bergamot, the scented sage, so that all would appear as normal as possible. Then they got on their bikes and rode off the property.

Behind them the bruised spirits rose and shook themselves from a long uneasy sleep.

Two nights later his mother died. She just crumpled in front of his stepfather at a dance. He hadn't been there to see it but could still play it over in his imagination: his mother sauntering up, smiling with all of her heart in her eyes. His stepfather reaching out to hold her in his awkward but tender way, and then his own smile suddenly dying as she slipped down his body to the dance floor.

In rational waking moments, he understood that it was her weak heart that killed her, a birth defect no one before had detected. But swimming breathless just below the surface was the voice he couldn't shake, the one telling him that her death and their bad luck and the unearthing of those ancient skeletons were all entwined.

4

$\mathcal{E}$arl McKay sat at the kitchen table with Pop. It was the first Sunday in January, and Earl hadn't drawn a sober breath since just before Christmas. He'd staggered on snowshoes through a blizzard and pulled a hip flask from his jacket pocket. He proceeded to add "a little juice" to two stained coffee mugs. His hand shook as he poured the whiskey.

Lonny turned away. He took off his glasses and tossed them on top of the refrigerator. He went to the kitchen sink, where he loudly ran the tap and vigorously scraped caked-on eggs and crud off a black frying pan.

"I just wrote a letter to my daughter," said Earl. "It was her birthday a couple of weeks back. Time for a little celebration."

Even with his back to Earl, Lonny could hear the pleading tone of a weak man. A man who was the total opposite of Pop LaFrenière.

Pop was polite. Sometimes his politeness to people who didn't deserve it drove Lonny crazy. He watched

24

him get up from the table, go over to the stove, come back with the fresh pot of coffee.

"I didn't know you had a daughter, Earl," he said, pouring coffee into their whiskey.

"She's just turned seventeen years old, and that's about how long it's been since I've seen her."

Lucky for her, thought Lonny. He ran hot sudsy water into the sink.

"Well, well," said Pop sympathetically. "That is too bad. Children are a comfort." After a long pause, he added, "I don't know what I would have done after my Margaret died if it hadn't been for Lonny here."

Behind the clattering of dishes, the two men fell silent. Lonny felt an old pain rise in his heart. For Pop. For himself. For the woman they had both loved. Here he was, almost eighteen years old, and still, even in his waking life, the damn tears could come. They rolled from his eyes and fell through soap clouds into the dishwater.

When he was very small, before Pop, there had just been the two of them. Mom and him. Now there was just two again. Pop and him. Funny how life works out.

He often had memories about the small apartment back in Winnipeg. Now he realized that his mother hadn't been much more than a teenager. She chain-smoked back then. He remembered her thick silky hair pulled into a high ponytail. Standing on her lap, in his bare feet, the smoke from her cigarette curling up from the ashtray behind them, he'd put his hands on her cheeks, smoothing them, smoothing her hair, then reach his arms around and hug her. He could clearly remember her smell. She always smelled of cigarettes. Cigarettes and shampoo. And she always hugged him back, fiercely.

He also remembered the first time he saw Pop. He stood like a large bear in the doorway of their apartment. Then he took them out to McDonald's. He bought Lonny those little cookies. Two boxes. One for now. The other for later.

His mother had answered a personal ad in the newspaper. *Widowed farmer, no children, looking for companionship. Possible relationship. Children welcome.* The rest, as they say, was history.

Before Earl left, he pulled the letter to his daughter out of his pocket and placed it with drunken grace on the table. "Going back up to my little place now. Don't worry about me. Storm's subsided from the look of it. But would one of you mind dropping this off in the mail when you're in town?"

"Lonny will be glad to do it," offered Pop. "You'll do that for Earl, won't you, son."

"Yes," he said, noting that it didn't have a stamp. He would have to make a special trip from the high school to the post office downtown. On his lunch break. Most of which would be taken up with jazz band practice. Playing the four-hundred-dollar guitar that had been his extraordinary seventeenth-birthday present from his perpetually broke stepfather. Never mind, he'd buy the goddamn stamp.

"I'd be grateful," said Earl, looking up at him with watery weary eyes.

Earl went out the door, tied on his snowshoes, and, whistling tunelessly, staggered off into the snowy hills again.

On Monday, Lonny meant to mail the letter, but band practice went overtime. And Tuesday and Wednesday and Thursday he went right from school to his job, at Petro-Can. Friday, Pop came around to the school at lunchtime to say that Earl had caught a really bad virus, and he'd just had to admit him to the Valley View Health Centre. Saturday, Sunday, and Monday, Earl continued to get worse. Tuesday, something went wrong with his heart. Wednesday, he developed pneumonia, and then things truly went from bad to worse. The following Monday he died.

Lonny still had the letter in the inside pocket of his jacket. He pulled it out frequently to look at it. He liked her name: Alexandra Marie Sinclair. He liked the way it sounded. What could Earl possibly find to say to a daughter he'd never taken care of, never even met? He couldn't send it now But he couldn't just throw it away either. Finally, he put Earl McKay's last letter to his daughter into the drawer beside his bed. And that was that.

5

When Alex's Cree grandfather was a young man, he came back, disillusioned, fearful, and a little bit crazy, from World War II. "My reaction to that," he told her once, "was to go *way* far up north. Lose myself in the bush. Had a trapline there. Trapped mostly white arctic fox, some beaver, the occasional lynx. That first winter I remember months and months of snow that cleaned out my spirit. I remember drinking tea made from boiled snow water. And smoking kinnikinnik with a man who told me to pay close attention to my dreams. They would tell me things, he said, that would be important to my life. So then I stayed up north. I stayed for nineteen years. I was a lonely man back in that time. Sad in my heart. And then, finally, my dreams led me to your grandmother."

The night before the letter arrived, the stranger's letter, she had a vivid, confusing dream.

Down a hill, by a lake, she watches Grandpa fishing. Talking to himself, his voice rising and falling, a soft drone. He casts off a perfect line that catches the sun and wind in midair, like spider silk. She follows the line over the lake. She tumbles with it as the air cools, then suddenly freezes into winter. And then she is tracking her father through the sloping light of January. He wears Grandpa's old bear-paw showshoes that move swiftly over the crusted snow. She wades through the tracks because her bare feet will not hold her on the surface. The snow sings around her: Vanished, vanished, vanished.

She woke up suddenly, feeling empty and cold, and turned her face on her pillow to look at the glowing frost patterns on the window. What had she been dreaming? Yes, she remembered! She saw Grandpa clearly, just as if it were only yesterday and not one entire long year since he had died and disappeared from this planet.

Strangely, too, there was her father. And why would he be there? But then it wasn't exactly a dream about him. It was a dream about his absence.

All the letters he had ever sent to her, half a dozen, nested like hollow eggs in a small brown box on her window ledge. Addressed in his faded scrawling handwriting to Miss Alexandra Marie Sinclair. Through the years each letter had scratched at the faint tracings of his life. The pale postal stamp on the first letter said *Calgary, Alberta.*

She's six years old. Her mother leans against the doorway of the kitchen in a long white bathrobe and watches her open the letter. That night she can't sleep, she is so excited. In the morning, her mother makes her put it away. In its proper place. But she keeps stealing it out to look at it.

And the next letter? No return address again. But the postmaster's stamp read *Indian Head, Saskatchewan.*

No, you can't write back to him. How would he get it? He's probably moved on anyway.

Dear Daddy, I can't send this letter. But I'm writing to you anyway. It's wintertime. Are you cold? Why don't you come and see me? You could stay at Grandpa's house. He has an extra bedroom. Your loving daughter, Alexandra Marie Sinclair.

Letter number three came from Medicine Hat.

Dear Alexandra Marie, How are you? I am fine and working at a ranch. Have a happy 10th birthday. Sincerely, Earl McKay.

Dear Father, I know you won't get this letter. But I'm sending it anyway. Why don't you ever ever ever come and visit me? Are you mad at me? I'm mad at you. Please send me another letter or I will never speak to you ever again. Your daughter, in case you have forgotten, Alexandra Marie McKay-Sinclair.

In the fourth letter he had moved on to Lethbridge. Moving. Always moving.

She's sitting in a restaurant with Mom and Auntie Francine. Her aunt is going on about how that "nomad" was thirteen years older than her mother— unlucky thirteen—and about how he was always full of schemes and big ideas. And her mother, clinking perfect unpolished nails against a water glass, tells Francine, "Well, I loved him. Once."

An old argument. As old as his letters to her.
In his fifth letter he was back here, in Manitoba.

Dear Alexandra, I'm here in the Lacs des Placottes Valley. Staying for a while. It's a beautiful day. I like it here. Say hello to your mother if she cares for me to remember her. I hope you have a good summer. Take time, as they say, to smell the roses. Wild ones, I figure, are the best. Take care, my girl. And always look the world straight in the eye. Sincerely, Earl McKay.

Dear Dad, I am . . .
Dear Dad, How are . . . ?
Dear Dad, I don't know what to say to you. . . .

And in his sixth and final letter, he'd gone back to Lethbridge.

Her mom brought in the morning mail. She was spending longer than usual in the hallway. In the kitchen, Alex and Auntie Francine were playing cards. Francine shook with laughter, so pleased with herself for putting down two one-eyed jacks.

"Did I ever tell you about that first time I saw all three of them?" Grandpa had asked Alex many times, always just before he launched into, "Your grandmother and her two little girls. Your mother was so small and delicate, and Francine like a gawky bird with those big eyes. Just like I'd seen them in my dream. I had to rub the cobwebs out of my own eyes. There they were, all three of them, standing outside the Hudson's Bay Company Store, at Caribou Post. That was 1964. Your grandmother was newly widowed. But she had a brilliant red ribbon in her hair. And she wore it proudly, like she owned the world. I see her even now"—he'd close his eyes—"always that red ribbon. And I knew I had found my heart's home."

As he spoke, she would pore over this historical moment in his life, each detail standing brightly in her mind: the grandmother she never got to meet, Mom, and Auntie Francine, all of them so young in that faraway place.

Alex slowly began to pick up ten more cards, drawing out the agony. She loved playing this stupid game of crazy eights with her nutty aunt.

Her mom came back into the kitchen. In a low clear voice, she said, "Earl's dead." Her fingers trembled. She gripped the edges of thin letter paper. Francine's smile dropped like a stone in dark water.

Alex took a deep breath. She thought about Grandpa. She got silver-white flashes of the park that January night, of running through the snow, of the ambulance outside Grandpa's apartment block.

A second deep breath. Her mother pulling her into

her arms. "Your grandfather is dead," she whispered. A simple statement. *Your grandfather is dead.*

A third breath. Earl McKay was her father.

A fourth breath. Quietly, with wonder, she said, "Last night I dreamed about him dying."

"How?" said Francine, who didn't appear to have heard what she had just said. "What does the letter say, Jeanette?"

Mom folded and unfolded the letter. Finally, she tucked it in her pocket. "That he died of pneumonia."

"Pah!" Francine exclaimed, throwing up her hands. "If I know Earl McKay, there's more to it than that."

"More to what? Mom? What's going on?"

"I can't believe you still haven't told her," Auntie Francine said with a kind of low, helpless rage. "You have a ridiculous attitude toward him, Jeanette. And you always have."

Alex's mom just stood, unanswering, perfectly composed, her Dene bones, her rich silken skin, her black hair pulled back with a four-directions beaded hair clip, her ears glinting with silver and turquoise earrings. "Always a lady, just like her mother," Grandpa used to say.

Francine grabbed up her sweater and coat and her car keys and said, "You're not going to read it to me, are you. If you want to be so stubborn and carry your pain around like it's some goddamn jewel, well, go ahead." Then she left. She was always leaving. Making abrupt exits. Her way of coping. But she always came back.

Alex said, "What haven't you told me, Mom?"

Her father was "a catastrophe," according to Auntie Francine. A series of catastrophes drove him away from home, away from them. First, he's laid off from his construction job. Next, he gambles away the rent money in a poker game. She is born three days later during the middle of a howling blizzard. When Grandpa discovers catastrophe number two and shames her father by covering the rent money, he comes one more time to the hospital to see her and her mom. Then he takes off. A few months later family friends say they've seen him up in Edmonton. "At least then your mother knew he was alive," said Francine, "not like some cat that didn't come home because it went out and got run down by a bus."

Sometimes she thought he was a criminal. Sometimes she thought he was an ordinary man. Most times she thought he was a coward. Still, she had longed for those letters. Hoarded them, kept them perfectly in the shiny wooden box, memorized them.

The afternoon snowlight outside the window was brighter than bright. It hurt the eyes. The sky burned blue straight up to the heavens. Beyond that, the cosmos, the darkness of space. But down here, on planet earth, another winter day.

Mom looked out the window. Her eyes suddenly teared up. "Every letter he ever sent you," she said carefully, "you've kept like a sacred thing."

"Mom, that's all I ever had of him."

She turned to look at Alex. "Exactly."

"What kind of an answer is that? I was six years old when I got his first letter. Mom, I could barely read. You could have kept it from me. But you didn't. You gave it to me. You read it to me." And you allowed me to get sick with excitement, she thought, but she would never say it. There are some things you should not say out loud.

"Alex, he could never stick to anything for long. I've told you this before. But he loved you . . . in his own way."

She had one memory of him. Of a shadowy man coming to her crib one night when she was crying. Of him picking her up and singing to her. But in this memory she's about three years old, so it was probably Grandpa. Or maybe she just dreamed it. Or maybe she just wanted it to be real.

Alex felt her hands begin to tremble. "Where do you get this fantasy about him loving me?" She stopped right there. The word *fantasy,* she could plainly see, flipped over her mother's heart.

Mom said, her eyes huge with sadness, "Will you let me read *this* letter to you?"

The envelope, addressed to Miss Jeanette Sinclair, was from T. LaFrenière, Box 56, Lacs des Placottes, Manitoba. Inside was the letter and two other pieces of legal-looking paper. Mom carefully opened the letter again, placing it on the table, smoothing the crinkle lines, then lifted it and read aloud:

"Dear Miss Sinclair, This is a difficult letter to write. It concerns a man named Earl McKay, who, I understand, was your husband and the father of your daughter, Alexandra Marie.

"I regret to inform you that Earl passed away last week. He died of complications due to pneumonia. And he'd made sure, earlier, that I had your address. He did not want to trouble you with his funeral and wanted simply to be cremated. He also asked if I would straighten his affairs and effects after his death, and this is why I am writing. He left a will."

"A will?"

"Just wait," said Mom, waving her hand. "Let me get through this." She took a breath, swallowed hard, and, hand over her heart, began again.

"My involvement with him started when he came looking to buy a few acres of my land. At that time, I was not ready to sell, but he stayed for a few days, helping out around the place. Then he left, and I thought that was the end of it.

"But he returned about a year later. And as he was willing to negotiate a very generous offer, I took him up on it. I needed the money, you see.

"He didn't appear like a man of any means at all. In actual fact, Miss Sinclair, he was something of a lone wolf. But perhaps you already knew this, and other things about him. I discovered that he was also a hard worker. So I guess that's how he'd conducted his life all along.

"He lived for a few months in the house trailer that he'd borrowed from me and pulled onto the land. But by winter he'd had a well dug and hadn't he gone and completed building a fully winterized four-room cabin overlooking the lake there!

"It was a shame that he never really got to enjoy it. But then life plays funny tricks sometimes, doesn't it. Just when you think you're away, you find out you're not.

"Anyway, the upshot of this is that his last will and testament leaves this cabin and the property to his daughter, Alexandra Marie."

"My father left me land? And a cabin by a lake?"

"There's more," said her mom. "He evidently left you some money."

"Money?"

"He left you almost seventeen thousand dollars."

"Seventeen *thousand*?"

"Evidently. Yes. To cover yearly property taxes. Other expenses. It takes a lot of money to run a place." She took another breath, held it, let it go like a thin prayer. "It's all in his will. Here, read for yourself."

The words blurred. It was all very legal. She looked at the paper that gave over this piece of her father's life. She ran her fingers over the document. She felt as if she were holding air.

Alex thought of all the times when she was younger, when Mom had gone back to school and was so strapped for cash. It was Grandpa who was there to help out. He bought their groceries and paid their rent. He'd shuffle through the door, practically every Saturday afternoon, grocery bags bouncing against his lame leg, and say, "Now, Jeanette, stop that studying for a while and take a rest. Let's make a little room on the table there. I noticed a special on oranges and chicken legs this week."

He would push aside all her mother's accounting texts and notebooks that she bent so feverishly over every night, long after Alex had gone to bed. Then he'd sit down at the little kitchen table. If Alex was sitting in one of the chairs, he'd reach out and pull it, with her on it, skidding up alongside him.

"Alexandra," he'd say, "what do you know for sure today?"

"Nothing." She'd giggle, because that was what she was supposed to say.

"Nothing! Well, we'd better fix that."

It was Grandpa who was there if either of them got sick. He was there for outings to the museum, to movies, to plays, to the sun-dappled hiking trails at La Barrière Park. And those camping trips to Spirit Lake, a lake so deep no one had ever found the bottom. He was there for science projects. He was there for every birthday. He knew all her favorite songs. And from the time she was a very little girl, he never made her feel bad for wanting the things she couldn't have.

Alex reached out and covered her mother's hand with her own. "Don't cry. . . . Mom? You're crying over somebody who isn't worth it."

Mom leaned back, pulled a Kleenex out of her cardigan sweater, blew her nose. "It's just that . . ." She looked away. Then looking straight at Alex again, fresh tears flowing down her face, she said, "I have so many things to be sorry for."

"You?" said Alex, sad and bewildered. "What have *you* got to be sorry for?"

One time, she and Grandpa were sitting together on Auntie Francine's scratchy brown sofa. It was Sunday, and just the day after she'd gotten a letter from her dad, the one that referred to the roses.

The two sisters, her mother and Auntie Francine, whispered together as they prepared dinner in the kitchen.

"Paul," Francine had said to Grandpa, "just relax. Let us fix you some tea."

In the kitchen, Auntie Francine, her eyes as cagey as a wolf's, listened to the rise and fall of her sister's voice. Alex could see them, positioned as she was in the middle of the sofa. She was twelve and a half years old.

"Jeanette," Francine finally interrupted, "why do you keep going over all these old hurts and hopes and memories? You're like a broken record. Just let go of him, for heaven's sake."

She raised her eyes briefly, saw Alex looking at them, then lowered her voice so that Alex could only pick out the odd word above the Disney show about bears that Grandpa was watching with rapt and respectful attention.

But she knew, without even hearing the conversation, that her mother's depressed mood had something to do with the letter. The sadness was always there, pervading their house each time another letter arrived. She felt guilty for wanting those letters when her mother got nothing. She felt even more guilty for wanting to know her father. To know who he really was.

"Why . . . ?" she began, and then stopped.

"Why what, little bug?" Grandpa asked, pulling his eyes away from the bears.

"Why," she said again, in a very low voice, "aren't there any photographs of him . . . of my dad?"

Grandpa slipped his arm around her. "She tore them up. Every one of them."

"Why?" she ventured.

"Someday she'll tell you. When she's ready."

He rocked her quietly for a while as she thought about this. A few minutes later he said, "We all make our mistakes. And we live with them. We all do the best we can. Things work out. Usually. You're going to be just fine, Alex. And your mom's going to be fine, too. Stop worrying so much. Who's my girl?"

"I am," she said, smiling up at him.

"And don't you ever forget it," he said, holding her tighter.

Now her mother, sitting still as a widow, seemed emptied out of tears. For this moment at least. Alex got up and moved around the table, put her arms around her neck, rested her face against her smooth strong-boned cheek. "I love you very much," she said fiercely. At this moment she hated her father very much.

Her mom let out a little ragged breath, patted Alex's skin. "I'll be fine, honey. I'm just in a bit of shock. This has all been such a surprise."

Alex went up to her room and sat on the edge of

her bed. What would Grandpa think about all this? From her bedside drawer she took out a fresh sheet of notepaper and a pen and started to write.

Dear Grandpa, I'm writing this letter to you even though you're dead. You once told me that life is full of surprises, and sometimes the good ones and the bad ones get all bunched up together. Well, I think this is one of those times. If you are watching over me, like I felt you were that night in the park, the night you died, then I guess by now you know that I dreamed about him dying.

She gripped her pen. Did she see her father's face in that dream? *He was something of a lone wolf,* Mr. LaFrenière's letter had said, *but perhaps you already knew this, and other things about him.* Other things? What other things? Her head hurt. She felt cold. She pulled Grandpa's ratty old blue sweater off the back of her chair and put it on. It still carried the memory of their camping trips and woodsmoke. She continued to write:

He's left me land in the country, Grandpa. And a cabin. And seventeen thousand dollars. That's one thousand dollars for every year of my life. Every year that he didn't bother to try and be part of. Can you imagine that? Did he actually plan it this way? Did he really think that this would be some kind of terrific payoff?

This is a terrible gift. I want it. And I hate it. And I hate him. What am I going to do? Loving you with all my heart, Alex.

She sat back and folded the letter in four. Then she held a match to it and burned it so that no one else would ever read it, so that the words she had written would become a living secret inside her heart.

She got off the bed and removed the sweater, her shirt, her jeans. She looked at her hands, her body, her legs in the mirror. She stood there in her cotton underwear and thought, Who is this big, tall person?

She solemnly reviewed her mother's long bones and dark eyes, eyes that flew back to her Dene grandmother and then back and back and back, through thousands of unimaginable years on one continent. Then she reviewed Auntie Francine's smooth nose and pretty lips. And then her own hair; neither her mom nor her aunt had hair this color. Grandpa once called it buffalo hair.

"*Buffalo* hair? That's not very flattering, Grandpa."

They were in a boat in the middle of deep, mesmerizing, well-named Spirit Lake. She cast off a line, hoping for a big fish, and Grandpa said, "The buffalo has a beautiful dark reddish brown coat. Same color as your hair. And he's a powerful animal. Someday you'll meet somebody. And when you meet him, you'll think about this day. Because he'll have the gift of buffalo medicine. Do you know what that is?"

She shook her head.

"One time, just after your grandmother died, I'd been feeling sad. The doctor gave me pills for my nerves. They made me feel worse. I couldn't sleep. I couldn't eat. I was fixated on your grandmother's image. On the fact that I had lost her. I couldn't enjoy anything. Not the blue sky. Or my garden. Or the birds singing. All I thought about"—he closed his eyes—"*continually,* was what I had lost. Then, one night, I dream about a buffalo. The buffalo is the Creator's most precious gift to the Native people. And this buffalo is magnificent, except for one thing. It has a lame leg. Well, it limps right up to me and bellows, '*You!*'

"'Holy smoke!' I say, and I jump back about ten feet, but I can still feel its hot, hot breath on my face."

"You have a lame leg, Grandpa," she reminded him.

"I didn't." He looked at her. "Not before I had that dream." He paused. "But when I wake up, guess what!" He slapped his leg. "A twinge of pain. Right here. Right in that same leg as that lame buffalo."

"Grandpa," she said sternly, "you were imagining things. You have arthritis. Everybody knows that."

He shifted in the boat and looked behind him, as if the fish might be listening. Then he leaned forward and whispered, "That buffalo brought me strong medicine. I know it for a fact. I know it as sure and solid as this old blue boat we are sitting in. Unhh-huh. First, I threw away my pills. Then I started to notice things. My garden, that year, grew the biggest potatoes ever. I had such an abundance of potatoes, it made me laugh. And then I began to see your grandmother in your mother and in your aunt. Different little things they'd say and do reminded me of all the gifts of her life. And now I see her in the way you move your hands, little bug. And I feel grateful."

He looked away down the lake, and for the first time in her life she thought about the fact that they wouldn't just go on and on like this forever. Grandfather and granddaughter out fishing in a boat on a lake so quiet that the smallest of sounds became magnified.

"So how would I know," she whispered, "when I saw that person? That one who is supposed to have the gift of buffalo medicine."

"You'll know." With every small movement, the arms of his nylon jacket swished and sang against the side of the boat. "Tell him howdy for me." He smiled into the water and wiped at a sly tear that betrayed him, one that tumbled down his face. His short silver-and-black hair. His red cap that said *Tansi Lumber.*

Water lightly slapped the boat. Suncaps blinded her, and now her heart felt heavy with the weight of his inevitable absence. She was ten years old, and she wanted to say something to make this day better. So she said, like she really believed all this stuff he'd been telling her, "So how do you know it will be a he?"

"Ahhhh!" he teased, breaking the stillness out on the water. "Did I say 'he'?"

In the last six years of his life, Grandpa often spoke like that. As if he knew he wouldn't be around forever, and it was important that she know that after he was gone, life would still hold a potion for miracles. He wanted her to believe that. If you could just get hold of the formula, you could make something terrific out of everything, and stop yourself from being scared and screwed up and confused.

"What is this?" he asked one time, rolling in his

hand the smooth stone that always sat in the middle of his kitchen table.

"It's a stone," Alex replied, knowing full well that this was a very tricky question.

Grandpa chuckled and nodded his head.

The stone sat on his table for years. It didn't change in all the years she looked at it—round and gray with cloud-colored flecks.

"A rock can't have feelings," she said to him one day as they walked along a trail in the woods behind their tent at Spirit Lake.

"I see," he said, swatting at his arm. "Can a mosquito have feelings?"

"Only if you hit it."

"Then it would be dead. It would have no feelings."

"Grandpa, if a rock has feelings, then how come you have a captured rock at your house?"

He laughed and put his hand over his heart and said, "I asked it if it wanted to come home with me."

"Ahhh! You didn't do that!"

"I did! I asked it!"

And another day, "A rock can't tell time," she told him. "Don't tell me that a rock can tell time."

"It's smarter than time."

"Don't tell me that!"

"A simple rock can tell if it's day or night. Hot or cold. Summer, spring, winter, or fall. And a rock remembers things."

"What things?"

"Things like, for instance, this rock here, sitting on the table. Say it's time for me to have lunch. Well, while I'm having my tomato-and-cheese sandwich, this rock is remembering that time on the prairie when a buffalo came by and peed on it."

Alex laughed and laughed, and thought about this image, and laughed some more. "Grandpa," she said, giggling, "that's very rude."

"Over here or back there," he said, "two hundred years ago or today, it's all the same to a rock."

Three weeks before he died, he asked her, "What's this?" He placed the cold stone in her hand.

"It's your rock, Grandpa."

"No, it's yours," he said, adding, "yours to take care of. And notice how your hand is bigger than it used to be."

A rock. A simple rock.

She picked up the rock that now sat on her desk. She rolled it around in her hand and fingered all the places where it was rough and then smooth.

"Grandfather," she said to the rock, "what am I going to do?"

Then she put down the rock. She dressed again. She calmly phoned Serena and, with all of her dignity, told her about her father dying, about the will, the money, the cabin, and the land.

"What an *unbelievable* gift," said her friend. Her friend since they were both little bugs.

"I'll be right over," Alex told her solemnly. Downstairs, she carefully lifted her coat and scarf from the front-hall hook and strode three and a half blocks down their snowy street to see her.

Serena, now almost six feet tall, like Alex, and, like

her, more curvy than bony, opened the door. She said, "I'm sorry about your dad." She threw her arms around Alex. "I'm so, *so* very sorry. I know you never met him, but you wanted to. I know you wanted to."

Alex pulled away and shrugged her shoulders. "It doesn't matter anymore."

"You don't mean that. Of course it matters." She led Alex down the hall to her totally pink bedroom. It had a large and wonderful brilliant blue-and-green papier-mâché frog that hung by a cord from the ceiling—Serena's touch, not her mother's. "But now," Serena said, "now at least you have something."

"I suppose so," Alex responded miserably.

Serena started to laugh, her whole body shaking. "You *suppose* so? You're so weird. Who else in my life would react like the world's coming apart when they've just found out that they're practically an heiress."

"It's too complicated to explain," said Alex, feeling angry and helpless and guilty.

"Oh," said Serena, a little too lightly. "That's fine. Another time."

Alex now was sorry she came over. Sorry she ever told Serena about it.

6

*L*ast year, in eleventh grade, she and Serena had had that falling out. It was a couple of months after Grandpa's death. And, she could now admit, it was over something really stupid. The rock held a place of honor in her heart, but there had been many other things once belonging to Grandpa that she had latched on to.

Serena had borrowed his pen, now Alex's, and lost it. And it was just a pen, after all. One of those cheap drugstore ones that would have run out of ink after about three months. Yet she couldn't believe how angry she felt when Serena casually told her that it had been lost.

"I guess it fell out of my bag," she said. "My God, Alex, we're not talking about a religious relic. It was just an ordinary pen."

"It was his pen," said Alex icily, "that he wrote with. He wrote his last grocery list with that pen."

"*Grocery* list?" Serena wrinkled up her pretty nose. "Did you keep that, too?"

"Don't be ridiculous," said Alex, angrily turning away, shoving books, papers, binders into her backpack. The grocery list, in a very shaky hand, said *bananas, eggs, six muffins.* It was still pressed between the pages of the last paperback book he ever read.

Serena heaved a big sigh. "When are you going to stop all this crazy stuff and get on with your life?"

"I beg your pardon?"

"I can't talk to you," said Serena. "And you obviously don't want to talk to me, so I'm out of here."

"Fine," said Alex. "That's absolutely fine with me."

They didn't talk to each other for three months. And then Serena came back into her life. She arrived at her front door with an apology in the form of a bottle of cola, a bag of chocolate creams, and a double-cheese pizza.

And they never again talked about the pen.

7

They were colorless and odorless. Lonny sensed
them pressing against his bedroom window. Or standing in the darkest part of his room. Once, before
waking up, he felt something heavy on his chest. When
he opened his eyes, he discovered that he couldn't
move. Not his arms or legs or even his head. He lay
there, pinned by their weight. Sometimes he felt as if
a column of darkness had entered his body.

He was eleven years old.

Pop asked, "Are you sad?"

Of course I'm sad. I've killed my mother.

Pop would sit like a lost man at the edge of Lonny's
bed, a sandwich in his big hand. It would drip ketchup
onto the floor, and neither of them would bother to
clean it up.

Whenever Lonny thought back to that time, the
image of Pop and his sad midnight sandwiches
haunted his memory. That, and the ghosts of the
Ancients that lurked between the smells of burned
toast and unwashed clothing and growing dust. They

were silent when he was awake. But he grew to be afraid of sleeping.

He would hear water gurgling. He'd stand, in his dreams, on the LaFrenière homestead, a place he'd stopped visiting in his waking life. At his feet, an old spring would bubble up, the water trickling through a clearing in the woods all the way down to the lake. He'd drop down and lie on his stomach and drink thirstily from the spring, from the golden water that came from its source deep in the dark earth.

But always their voices came in the wind, pulling him away from some unnamed longing. "Sorrowwwww," they whispered through the pretty poplar leaves.

When Lonny turned twelve, the ghosts went away. He wasn't exactly sure what made them do that. He woke up one morning and was aware of a happy feeling for no special reason.

"Did you sleep well, son?" Pop asked, pouring hot chocolate out of a battered pot into Lonny's mug.

"Yep, I did." Lonny bent his head over the mug, slurping the hot liquid. He was trying to remember his dreams of the night before but found that he couldn't. They were, somehow, blocked. This, he decided, was a good thing.

The shadowy figures left the house. He imagined them floating back to Medicine Bluff, light and free. Occasionally, with a flicker, like a match struck in a moonless room, he thought about them and panicked. But he found that he could then push them away. Lock them out. And dream of nothing in particular.

Earl's death shook him. The dreams began full force again, but different this time. Always it was his mother, coming to him again and again in his dreams. She became less human and more spirit. She'd land delicately at the side of his bed, all snow and ice and feathery white fringes. She'd blow on his face as if she were the north wind. She would whisper, "Let the spirits dance. The land will wake up and tell you things."

What things? he asked with his mind. Every single time, he'd wake up to find himself as immobilized as that rusty snow-mounded wagon wheel that rested against the shed outside in the January darkness.

He tried talking to Robert about his dreams. Robert sitting in the cafeteria, his head full of hockey scores and daydreams of Tammy Martel, who still wouldn't sleep with him even though she'd done it with just about everybody else, Lonny included.

"What?" he said when Lonny was in midstream, middream. Then he laughed nervously. "That's *weird* shit, man."

"Yeah, weird." Lonny laughed, too.

After that, day after day went by with Robert talking on and on about nothing. Lonny let him talk and could tell that he was relieved no mention was made of his mother's spirit again.

He sleepwalked through his days, nudged by dreams, getting *A*'s and *B*'s with his mind half-awake. His English teacher, Miss Samson, handed him a paper he'd done on a poem by Dylan Thomas. "Good work, once again, Mr. LaFrenière," she said, and then frowned at the bags under his eyes. "I hope you're planning on going to university next year."

At the beginning of February. Robert said he was bored. "Everybody's bored, Lon." he said, "and that's because it's winter. And so we've got to do something about it."

He suggested they round up some Ski-Doos and a few people and go down to the old LaFrenière place and have a party. "Come on, Lon," he urged. "You've been all weird lately. And you need cheering up. And I'll bet not a single person has been down there since Earl kicked the bucket. So what'll it hurt?"

"I don't want to go down there," said Lonny.

But Robert wasn't listening, and he was so fired up, there was no stopping him. A couple of days later, people were coming up to Lonny in the halls at school. By Saturday night, nineteen people showed up at the top of the snowed-in trail, piling out of cars, unloading snowmobiles off the backs of family trucks. They showed up with cases of beer. tequila, gin, and cheap wine. It was fiercely cold, and the snow was waist deep in places. A caravan of lights wound down through the bush, everybody yelling and laughing past dark, silent winter trees.

At Earl's cabin, Tyler Lakusta, giggling like he was already drunk, pulled off his leather mitt, fumbled under his jacket and layers of sweaters for his wallet. While somebody shone a flashlight, he used his bank card to gentle the lock on Earl's door. It was easy. And it was wrong.

Charlene McLean had brought candles, and she

pulled off her boots at the door and told people they had to wait outside until they were lit. And when they finally did go in, it felt as if they were entering a church, candlelight flickering up the walls. Lonny half expected to see Earl laid out in a coffin in a suit even though he'd been cremated last month.

Charlene, her thick black hair hanging down her back in a single braid, opened her arms up wide and threw them around Lonny and yelled, "Surprise!"

And then everybody sang "Happy Birthday," and all he could do was stand there, stunned, because his eighteenth birthday wasn't until next week, but this was his party, obviously, and Robert had planned it all.

Later as the woodstove and all the bodies inside heated the cabin up, people got loud and drunk. Robert and John Tessier and Curt Mason and Morgen Thiessen staggered outside and stood in a snowdrift and pulled down their pants and mooned the moon. Tyler lured Marianne Neufeld off to Earl's bedroom, where she threw up in his lap.

Charlene came and sat beside Lonny on the living-room floor. She offered him a cold marshmallow from a bag she'd ripped open with her teeth.

"Hey, Charlene," he said softly.

"Hey, Lon. Are you having a good time?"

He shivered and looked at her glowing face. He'd known her ever since they were in second grade. All of them, all of the girls—Charlene, and Tammy Martel and Marianne Neufeld and Sherry-Lynne Baker and Jen "the Bird" Nightingale—had gone from wide-eyed seven-year-olds into golden-lidded women, it seemed, overnight. And now they seemed like strangers.

"Thanks for the candles," he said. "They look nice."

She drew a circle in the dust on Earl's floor. She turned to him, her warm eyes drawing him in. "You into this stuff?" And she went on. "Circle of life? Medicine wheels? Some eternal plan?"

"Not me." He smiled. "I'm just a bad godless boy. But my mom was. She had a gift for life. She could even see light . . . on trees."

"You mean like their auras?"

"I guess. Man, am I drunk," he went on, embarrassed.

"No, you're not," said Charlene.

He shrugged. "People think you're a fruit loop when you talk about stuff like that."

"Lonny"—Charlene put her arm around him, resting her head on his shoulder—"don't you know what people think of you?"

He laughed. "What *do* they think of me, Charlene?"

"And I'm not including your girlfriends now," she said. "Because, let's be honest, you're hell to have as a boyfriend. But you are a great friend. You know that? You listen to people. You make them feel like they could be anything, do anything. That's a gift. That's a real gift."

"I do that?" he said in amazement.

"Yeah," she said, snuggling closer. "Boy, it's cold. Put your arm around me. Tell me something good."

Alex dreamed of snow. A small cabin. A shiny window. Her grandfather's hand along her back. "Look, Alexandra." Brilliant snow, brilliant sky. The top of a hill. And suddenly a raven, flying out of the woods, sunlight tipping its wings.

During the day she sat and doodled black rocks on her purple plastic binder and got memory flashes of her dreams of the night before. Strange dreams. Crackling sticks and coals. The soft plunk of snow hitting the bottom of an iron pot. The rattle of tin cups. Cold lips slurping tea. Soft voices. Clicking tongues. The monotone of a language that was an unfamiliar landscape—her grandfather and someone else. Inside her mind, inside her sleepy mind, she was an animal, curled in warm furred sleep, listening to the blizzard outside batter and whine against the cabin door.

She and Serena and Peter Shingoose went to a party at Andrea Larkin's. Peter drank a lot of tequila, and then she and Serena spent the rest of the night sitting with him in the bathroom. At one point he slid down into Serena's lap and told her, "You're a goddess. And I'm a sad Adonis. I think I love you." Serena laughed, hugged him close.

He didn't show up at school on Monday, and Serena wanted to go over to his house "to see if he's okay." Tuesday, he showed up with a rose for Serena. Wednesday, she and Serena had another huge fight.

The first time she ever noticed Peter Shingoose he was hoop dancing at a powwow at the Convention Centre. She'd hauled Serena along. It was three weeks after their patch-up over the pen incident, and Serena was still in a mood of atonement. The floors pounded. The drumbeats came right up through her feet to her heart and made her cry. She felt like a fool, but she couldn't stop the tears. They flowed nonstop. Serena, dry-eyed, was astonished by all the color and the rhythm, and then all at once she said, pointing, "That guy is in my drama class."

There was Peter out on the floor in full costume, all feathers and hoops. He danced like a gorgeous bird. Alex's palms began to sweat.

He came up to them later, flashing a bone white smile at Serena. Alex couldn't breathe, her heart was pounding so. He won't notice me, she thought at that very moment. He'll only notice Serena because she's so beautiful. Serena always has boyfriends. She doesn't give a damn if she's tall and big and powerful. She just looks them in the eye, and they fall like bricks.

"You have to act more confident," Serena had told her back in the ninth grade. "When you're made the way we are, it's the only way you're ever going to be

57

popular." This remark was coming from the same person who had pretended to paint them both with invisible paint when they were five, so they wouldn't be noticed on their first day of school.

Well, Serena can have him, she then thought, looking at a point past Peter's ear so she wouldn't have to look directly at him again. He's too good-looking anyway. He's probably just a big snob.

But, as it turned out, he wasn't. And for the past six months they had been a constant threesome.

It wasn't that Alex never had sort-of boyfriends. You hung out. They kissed you, stuck their tongues in your mouth, grabbed you, played stupid mind games, power games, wanted you to come home with them when their parents weren't there. It was all very boring. And they knew Alex was bored, and it scared them. She wasn't small, and she didn't want to stand around under somebody's arm and be popular. Maybe there was something wrong with her. They never moved her. Nobody moved her until Peter. She would write his name in the pattern of a heart and draw an arrow through it. She would think about him as she lay in bed at night, a slow fire creeping up between her legs, into her belly. She wanted him to touch her here. And here. And here. She could never let on to anybody, especially Serena, how he made her feel.

Serena and Peter walked together in the halls at school, and Serena's eyes were shiny with light, and Peter drew her close every time someone was looking.

"You don't even like her," Alex said to Peter a

week after this had been going on. Heavyhearted, as weighted as a mountain to the earth, she added, "You're just playing a big pretend game."

"I like her," said Peter, a big-eyed liar.

"She's not your type."

He folded his arms across his chest, shook his hair out of his eyes, stared hard at her, angry, proud, eyes glittering. "Since when do you get to tell me who I can go out with?"

Peter left notes for Serena on her locker. *Meet me later. Love you madly.* Then he wouldn't show up. Andrea Larkin told Alex, "Peter says you and Serena had a terrible fight. Are you okay?"

She took refuge in sleep. Snow drifted across the cabin floor. Grandpa and some other spirit sat right there. Right in the kitchen. In yellow chairs. Grandpa slightly smaller. The other tall and thin and old, like a large and baggy raven. White hair flowing over the collar of a too-big black overcoat. Both of them as still as stone, snow resting in delicate drifts on their shoulders.

In the waking world, Mom looked haggard and ashen. She was always upstairs in her office. She made tense phone calls. Tripped over boxes of waiting tax files. Dashed out to meet with clients. Drank too much coffee.

One late afternoon, the sunset slanting through the window onto her computer, she sat, face practically absorbed by the screen, and Alex reached out one hand to unknot the tension at the back of her neck.

"God, that feels good," said Mom, dropping her head. "You've got healing hands, kid."

Then, lifting her head, she pulled Alex down in the chair beside her, with a soft "C'mere." Arms came around her, holding her in place in a firm hug. "I want to talk to you about something. I've set up a trust fund for you. With the money Earl left. I didn't want to just leave it in a bank somewhere, hardly collecting any interest."

Alex squirmed away. She went and sat down on the futon with the gold-colored throw. Shivering, she drew the throw around herself. She thought she might be sick.

"Anytime I bring up the property or the money," Mom said, pushing a tired hand through her hair, "you run away." She turned back to her computer, squinted her eyes painfully.

Two days later, Francine stood in the middle of the parking lot at Wal-Mart, where she had just purchased another set of towels that she didn't need. "Alex," she said, poking the key into the car door, "she's worried about you. And, of course, she comes to me about it. Why do you two always pussyfoot around each other's feelings? For goodness' sake, your mother isn't that fragile."

When Mom brought the subject up again, Alex said she was tired. "And I have a headache," she added, watching her mother's face crumple in disappointment.

She turned, made her way up the stairs, and could feel her mother, below, still watching her. Then just as she reached the bedroom door, Mom called out,

"You're going to have to start making some decisions. Have you picked up your University of Manitoba application yet?"

"I'll do it tomorrow."

"Deadline for application is March the third."

"I know that, Mom. I said I'll do it."

Her walking-around visions were frost laced. In biology lab she delicately dissected a frog, and all the while, dancing green northern lights crackled and whispered and invaded her nostrils with ozone.

Standing in the middle of Harmony Drugs one slushy day, balancing a box of tampons in one hand and a bottle of hair spray in the other, she had a vision of her grandfather as a young man, dressed in caribou skins and wearing his red Tansi Lumber cap. He walked right past her and joined the old raven man, his spirit friend in the black coat, who floated down aisle four and pointed incredulously at his own image on the TV monitor.

It was almost one o'clock. She had a class first period in the afternoon. Her legs felt leaden as she made her way toward the front. She was startled to see Peter standing at the checkout counter.

He turned around, looked at her over his sunglasses, turned back to the flirty candy-colored cashier, handed over a few bills and some change, turned around again. This exchange was all very surreal, like a painting she once saw, in blazing southwestern colors, of a coyote driving a red convertible past lime green cactus plants.

He had a balloon coming out of his mouth that said, "Hey, baby, what's new?" The painting cost thousands of dollars.

"Want a ride back?" he offered, leaning against the checkout counter.

"No," she said.

"Sure you do. Please?"

In his car, on their way to school, the dream catcher on his rearview mirror swayed hypnotically back and forth.

"Can't we at least be friends?" he said at last.

She looked straight ahead.

"Things are in a mess," he said, adding softly, "I don't know what to do about Serena. I started something I can't handle. My life's one big lie. The only time I ever feel like myself is when I'm dancing."

"Peter," she whispered, turning her face away, "why don't you just grow up?"

In her dreams she searched beyond concrete and city noise and chalk-smelling school corridors, beyond weekends during which her arms ached from her part-time job at Cuppa Java, beyond history and English and chemistry tests, all requiring at least a *B*. She managed an *A* in two and scraped up a *B* in chemistry.

She went to bed earlier and earlier. Made her room a sanctuary. Burned sage and sweetgrass on a clamshell, lit candles. She meditated from the womb of her bed, pressing past ceiling to stars, trying to find her way. And then she slept the clock around and dreamed.

Out of the hill pokes tree branches and rocks and shiny tin cans, and her father's shirts like fluttering flags and all of his money. His pile of possessions keeps growing. They are an eyesore. They are a blot on the landscape. Grandpa, bent over, carefully shovels them over in the earth, mounding them into the hill. He straightens up, leans on his shovel, wipes tears from his eyes. More tears keep coming. He's watching someone who is running down the hill. And then she knows, even as she's dreaming, that she is the one who is running away. Running and running. "Stop!" cries the raven, flying at her back. "Turn around and face the mystery."

Auntie Francine, the family tea-leaf reader, unwittingly came the closest to guessing about her dreams and waking visions one Sunday evening.

She stared into Alex's porcelain cup, cradled like a half-moon between her hands. "I see a disconnection," she said, studying the pattern in the leaves, "between your head and your body."

"Where? I don't see it," said Alex.

"Right there." Francine's thin finger pointed.

Alex peered at something that, to her, resembled a crow flying off a leafy tree in search of something. Then she thought, No, it's not a crow. It's a raven. It's a big raven. It's a raven transformed. From something. Changing shape. Shape from an old man. Old Raven Man.

"Your dreams," Francine primly advised, looking up, "are trying to tell you something."

Alex's heart caught in her throat. She hadn't mentioned a thing to anybody about her dreams. And now she felt her whole body flush hotly. "I don't know," she said carefully, "what you are talking about."

"Why haven't you been out to see Earl McKay's property yet? Don't look at me that way. The cat's been out of the bag for quite some time. You'll find land," her aunt persisted. "And, apparently, a cabin." Reaching across the table, she took a firm grip on Alex's hand. "Listen. Those little letters you've been holding on to for so long aren't him. But what he's left you is something real and solid. That's the important thing. Aren't you even a bit excited over this? Little bug?"

Francine hadn't called her little bug for years. The sound of it, popping up like an old and long-lost friend, made her sit there wanting to stay proud while tears poured down her cheeks.

"You're a normal girl," Francine added softly. "You should be happy about such a gift."

"Why . . . ?" Alex wiped her tears away. More kept coming.

"What? Spit it out."

"Didn't he leave *anything* . . . to her? She's the one who took care of me. Paid all the bills. Did whatever she had to. And I know Grandpa helped a lot. So did you. But she was the one. . . ."

Now she was bawling. She wanted to stop. She couldn't.

Francine pulled up her chair and rocked Alex in her arms. "She's very happy for you," she said carefully. "You know that. All her life she's worked hard. And now she's built up her little accounting business, and she's happy. And she wants you to be happy, too. She wants you to live a normal life."

Alex pictured her intestines at this very moment. They were snarled and knotted and begging for mercy. What did Francine mean, *normal?* Was her father crazy? Was that why he ran off? Was she going crazy, too?

Behind them, the kitchen faucet dripped slowly. Each drop drummed into the sink. She could hear the swelling majesty of powwow drums as her heart broke again and again.

9

Serena's dad had, for the third time in the past two years, walked out on her mother. This time they all thought it was for good. Mrs. Fitzpatrick, apparently, was standing in her nightgown by the fish tank, sobbing inconsolably over their seven-year-old goldfish Fillet, who had, coincidentally, just died of dropsy.

"We gave him antibiotics and everything, but he died anyway. It is so gross," Serena said over the phone to Alex. "All bloated and bloody. Nobody wants to touch him."

This was her way of saying she was in pain. A family crisis to override any pain she had caused Alex over the past three and a half weeks.

"I'll be there as soon as I can," Alex told her.

It was the only day she had to register at the University of Manitoba. Accessing the registry system took an hour. Then it took forever to get her courses. But if you hung up the phone you were dead, so you had to stay on the line. In the end, she got most of the ones she wanted, with a couple of compromises. Three hours later she was finally able to go over to the Fitzpatricks' and deal with the fish, which looked as if it had exploded.

She made Serena toast and scrambled eggs with cheese and jalapeño peppers and brought it to her in her pink room, where they sat under her wonderful hanging frog.

"This is so nice of you," Serena said, her lower lip trembling. She picked away at the eggs, put down her fork, buried her face in her hands, and sobbed. And then, "Peter just broke up with me," she said finally. "I've tried and tried with him. I don't understand. I don't know why he doesn't love me."

10

*W*hen Pop, with sad pouchy eyes, finally got around to telling him, four months after the fact, that Earl had left the LaFrenière homestead to his daughter, two things happened.

One, he wanted Pop, for Pop's sake, to try to buy back the property.

"We could afford it," said Lonny. "Things aren't so bad now."

"Pretty soon you're graduating from high school," Pop said quietly, nodding his shaggy head. "It's less than a month away. Don't you have any plans?"

Here it was again, guilt money, and the guilt not even intended. "I'm going to stay out a year and work," said Lonny. "I'd rather do that. Really I would. I just don't know what I want. Not yet. You'd be wasting your money, Pop."

"But the money's there now," said Pop with a sidelong look, his eyes veiled with sadness, "and you're so smart." He rubbed the back of his big wrinkled neck and added, "And what's done is done. The land is sold. Won't you take this opportunity?"

"Pop," said Lonny softly, "you can't keep living your life for me."

"Who says I can't?" Pop gave him a quick bone-rattling hug.

It was so depressing. Pop was forty-eight years old. Working in a lumber store. Living in a crappy little house on a crappy little piece of land. He has no life, Lonny thought, and he deserves so much more.

Later, feeling off-balance and ill, he got in the truck and drove off in the dust over to Robert Lang's place. It was a night of long twilight at the end of May. The two of them wheeled through the blue shadows into town and got a twelve-pack of beer and a Jack Daniel's and a large bottle of cola. They parked by the lake, near the old dance pavilion, and proceeded, quietly, to get very drunk.

By around two in the morning, the moon hung over the water, and the sky was draped with the darkest blue. Robert slid down beside the truck, his knees poking up in the air, his hand fanning away a swarm of fish flies. "I got this memory that's been doggin' my ass ever since we were little kids," he said. "Remember that time, Lon, when you and me dug up that old mound?"

"Yes," said Lonny.

"Found those bones," Robert went on. "Damn, that was scary. You ever think about that?"

"Yes."

Robert nodded his head drunkenly and poured some

more Jack Daniel's into their cola bottle. "Wondered about that, with your Native ancestry and all. Been giving it some serious thought lately. Me and Charlene had a big long talk about your ancestry. And other stuff."

"You. And Charlene."

"Yep," he said, pointing up at the Milky Way. "She's into some very interesting stuff. She claims that those buggers up there see everything we do."

"What buggers?"

"The stars in the cosmos and shit. Look at them, man. They're *cooold*." He took a swig from the plastic soda bottle.

Lonny took the bottle from Robert. "Know who owns the LaFrenière land now? Earl's daughter. City girl. Lives in Winnipeg." He let the cola and Jack Daniel's slide and sting down his throat.

"His daughter." Robert nodded his head in a stunned way. And then, for quite a while, they listened to the lake slap and sigh along the shore. "So," he said quietly, "she's the one who's going to end up with the land that was supposed to be yours."

"Who cares," said Lonny grimly.

But that was a lie. The stars knew he was lying. They shone down colder than ever. And beside Robert, his best friend ever since childhood, he felt the loneliness of that lie.

By morning they'd moved down to the lake shore and were sprawled asleep on old blankets in the sand. Robert, who was the first to stir, shivered in the misty early morning chill and poked at Lonny.

"A raven took my T-shirt," said Robert.

"Bull!" Lonny sat up, giggling. He pulled on his cowboy boots and then tried to stand. He was still a little drunk.

"I'm not kidding." Robert grinned, looking at him with red puffy eyes. "Great big old raven stole my shirt. He was watching me, I swear. And then I catch him out of the corner of my eye. He's picking it up in his beak. And he flaps off with it. Bugger."

Lonny fell back in the sand and laughed some more.

"Robert," he said, patting his friend's back. "Don't tell me you're getting into some weird shit. Let's buy you a cup of coffee, man, and sober you up. Then we've got to get home. Pop's likely going crazy by now, wondering where I am."

They went into Deena's Deli and ordered two cups of coffee and a couple of burgers to go. They stood waiting by the big front window. The door swung open and shut, open and shut. The place was busier than usual, but Deena, her wild blond hair flying, her skinny hips held skinnier by faded jeans, her long freckled neck gleaming with sweat, came out of the kitchen at the back to deliver their order herself. She placed it on the counter, peered at them through her bangs, and said to Lonny, "Honey, you look a mess. Where have you been sleeping all night?"

"On the beach." Lonny grinned at his mom's old friend and then at Robert, who was smiling foolishly as Deena leaned over. Her breasts were compact and golden all the way down the front of her navy blue V-necked sweater. "How did you know we didn't go home?"

"I know everything there is to know about you and then some," she said, easing a couple of napkins into the bag that held their order. "And you didn't call home either." She raised her eyes, smiled, shook her head. "He called not more than five minutes ago. Looking for you. You want me to tell him you're on your way?"

"It's okay, Deena," Lonny said, chuckling. "We'll be home before you know it."

The day of his mom's funeral, it had been Deena who had comforted him, back home, as Pop lay in his room on the bed that he and Lonny's mom had shared for only four years. Pop was inconsolable, so full of grief that he couldn't stand up.

Lonny thought about how he saw Deena practically every other day. But he still couldn't talk to her about his mom. He couldn't because Deena carried her grief around, wore it close to the surface. It was visible in the way she wiped off the red-topped tables, her bony shoulder blades moving sharply beneath her thin knitted tops, beneath her honey-colored flesh. It was there, probably, when she groomed her horses, up the road from them, on that little piece of land she had lived on ever since her hippie days. It was there, he could plainly see, in every lonely look she gave to Pop whenever he shyly ordered the daily special.

He thought back to how, in the year following his mom's death, they saw less and less of Deena. And then one September day she'd come riding down the road on her horse. He had been sitting there, chucking rocks into the ditch. Across the way in the wheat field,

Pop was combining, sitting high in the air-conditioned cab, his total attention on getting another crop off the land before freeze-up.

It was Saturday. Lonny was supposed to be out on the land, helping. But when he wouldn't, Pop swore under his breath and left him lying facedown in bed, inhaling the smell of sour sheets.

Deena slid off her horse and left the animal to wander down and graze in the ditch. Lonny continued to chuck stones. He didn't even want to see her. That's how bad he felt. Maybe she'll go away, he thought. She's stupid, just stupid.

But she sat down in the grass beside him, her hands on her knees. "I'm sorry I haven't been around," she said. "I've been really busy."

Yeah, right, he thought. Liar, you big liar.

And then she said, "I miss her, too."

She moved closer. He felt her gently tug on the elastic that held back his hair until it was free, blowing in the hot prairie wind. He could smell an earthy perfume rising off her skin. She combed her fingers through his hair, her nails raking his scalp in a soothing way, and then she tied it back again.

"Your mom always liked you to wear your hair this way," she said.

"Robert," he told her, "that first day I met him? He was standing at the drinking fountain, and he told me I was an Indian."

Deena laughed. She had a wonderful warm musical laugh. "That's obvious," she said. "What did *you* say?"

"Nothing." Lonny grinned at her. "I stared him down. I made him look away and be ashamed. Nobody teased me about my hair after that. The girls wanted to touch it."

"I'll bet they did," said Deena, smiling into her open hands. "You have a way about you that's so much like her, you know. So much like your mom."

He sank his head down, felt his hair resting between his shoulder blades. "Yeah, well, I'm not her," he mumbled. "She's gone. And she's never coming back."

"Do you ever talk to your pop about this?"

"About what?" He lifted his head, gave her an angry look.

"About how you're feeling."

"I'm not feeling anything," Lonny said defiantly. "And Pop would be better off without me."

"Oh, don't say that," she told him, and the sun glanced harshly across her face, lighting it with a fierce white light. "You are all he has. You're his reason for getting up in the morning. He likes taking care of you."

It was a moment that stood out in his heart. To be all somebody has, to be their reason for getting out of bed, that was something you could hold on to—even if nothing else mattered.

Months of silence were replaced, after that visit with Deena, by a thousand little kindnesses. A floor scrubbed. A vase of blue prairie asters on the table. The black shoes Pop had worn to the dance the night Mom died were pulled out of the bottom of his closet, polished, the laces replaced, and left conspicuously beside his chair where he would find them.

And from Pop, a new hockey stick laid across Lonny's bed. A hand briefly hugging his shoulder as he sat doing his homework. The word *son* appearing in every single request: "Come to town with me, son." Or, "Help me with the chores now, son." Blessing him, pulling him away from his dark thoughts.

They left Deena's Deli, and he and Robert got into Pop's truck and ate their burgers, parked on the main street of the town of Lacs des Placottes. Its sun-soaked streets, its tall overhanging trees, the cheerful mall by the grain elevator, the farmers and their round wives, the John Deere dealership up the street, the bakery and all the pretty girls who worked there had seemed at first strange to him when he was a small boy, coming from Winnipeg.

Tammy Martel slowly made her way up the street, a white T-shirt skimming her navel, her little dark-haired brother leaping on the end of her hand like a trout fighting air.

"Hey, Tammy," Robert called out the window, slapping the side of Pop's truck. "C'mere!"

Tammy in a back bedroom at Tyler Lakusta's family cabin on Fatback Lake. An eleventh-grade drinking party with a mix of kids from all over the valley. Tammy, breathing underneath him, her hair smelling like vanilla. For weeks after, she would call him at home, show up at the gas station, arrange to sit beside him in band class, her slender hands moving like liquid up and down the strings of a bass guitar.

By then, he had moved on to Jen, her arms fragile as wings, her breath hot as July, who pulled him behind Petro-Can, where they both worked, and said, "I don't know where you think this is going, Lonny, but I'm tired of your bullshit. Talk to me."

"I don't know what you mean," he said.

"Sure you do," said Jen. "Do you think you can just go around getting involved with people's hearts and then walk around like you don't respect them?"

"What? What the hell have I done? Tell me what I did."

"You don't call me, that's what. Then, when you feel like it, you pick me up and take me to the quarry, and you pull out a blanket and a condom, and I'm supposed to be so damn impressed. Well, I'm sick of it. You don't love me. You don't talk to me. I'm just some . . . some *temporary distraction*. What the hell is wrong with you?" She stood there waiting for him to deny his guilt. But it was true what she said.

After a long terrible silence, in which he kicked at the ground and wished for it all to be over, she finally said, "You just like to screw me. That's all. No big deal. Nothing. I'm a *person*, Lon. Look at me." Big tears welled up in her eyes, rolled down her cheeks.

"I'm sorry. I'm really, really sorry. It's me, Jen," Lonny mumbled. "I'm sorry . . . for everything."

"Oh, yeah, you big jerk," she sobbed, her thin shoulders heaving. "Don't you ever touch me again."

Tammy Martel strolled toward the truck, Lonny's

side. Her baby brother broke free and crouched down in his little red rubber boots, his John Deere cap slapped on the back of his head. Lonny watched him scratch a beautiful iridescent green beetle out from between the cracks of the sidewalk and place it, helpless, on its back in the center of his palm.

"Hi," said Tammy, dangling one soft perfumed arm over the open window, her brunette hair a shiny cloud around her face.

Robert, face flushed, said, "What are you doing later?"

"Nothing much," she said casually, peeling away to glance back at her brother, who was now poking at the desperate beetle with a small stick. Lonny had to look away to keep himself from saying something.

"You want to do something later?" Robert asked Tammy.

"Like what?" she said flatly, shifting so that her arm almost touched Lonny's shoulder.

"We'll go to the drive-in. Okay?"

"Yeah, sure. Shane, we have to go. Are you finished torturing that thing?"

Shane looked up, grinned, swiped the dead beetle on his jacket.

"Bye," Tammy said softly to Lonny, and then she disappeared from the window.

Robert called after her, "I'll pick you up around seven!" And he watched, hopefully, for several seconds before he finally turned his head back to Lonny. "Did you see the way she looked at me? Did you? This is amazing. This is my lucky day, man."

"Yeah," Lonny said wearily.

After that, they went home, where Lonny tried to get used to the idea of the LaFrenière land now belonging to some spoiled-rotten city girl who didn't deserve it. And not to Pop, who did.

A month later he was still not used to the idea.

"Maybe she'll just not bother to show up," he said, taking his morning coffee out in the June sunlight to join Pop on the front steps.

Pop slowly sipped his coffee and looked up at the drifting clouds. "She'll be here," he said. "It's just a matter of time."

11

Mid-June and the morning of their graduation dance. She and Serena were going as each other's date. Sprawled on top of Alex's bed, they were doing their goddess thing. Alex painted Serena's toenails. Gypsy Gold.

Out of the blue, Serena opened her mouth and said, "If it were me, I'd sell the land, take part of the money, and spend it on a modest vacation to, say, oh—Brazil! Then I'd invest the rest in Serena's Catering Service. It's the *best* gift. No strings attached. Alex, why haven't you at least gone out there? You've had it for five months already. Don't you even want to see it? We could go together. Let's do that!"

Outside, the noisy traffic whined by. Serena dropped an orange section into her mouth and said, "Come on, it'd be fun."

Alex flicked bloodred, gold-flecked polish on Serena's toes. Flick. Flick. Flick. Skip a beat. Skip a breath. And a sudden image spun wildly in, crashing powerfully against her heart. A bone-shaped lake with the

hill of her dreams rising above. Grandpa and Old
Raven Man fishing at the rocky shoreline. Grandpa's
fish breaks the surface. Beads of water, flung from its
massive tail, arc far across the dark green skin of the
lake. It flips and dances and fills the sky. It's the mother
of all fishes, full of God and terrifying magic. Old
Raven Man suddenly sits down, laughing, his long
birdlike hands slapping his knees. Grandpa turns his
head. His lips form these unmistakable words: "Alexandra! It's time!"

She smeared the polish. This is not normal, she
thought. Normal people do not go around having
visions.

Serena rescued the pot of Gypsy Gold. "What?"
she said with a strange smile. "You look like you've
just seen a ghost."

12

She and Serena sat at their table at midnight. Purple and white balloons drifted across the floor. A few couples still danced under the dim lights. A scattering of people in the bathrooms were throwing up. Jason Lavoie swayed over to their table with Melissa Singarajah on his arm. He was very drunk, and she more or less held him up.

"Alex," he said, falling into a chair beside her. "Alex," he breathed again.

Melissa folded her arms and pretended to look at everybody dancing.

He sighed. "Alex, you're beautiful. Look at her, Melissa. Don't you think she's beautiful?"

"Are you trying to say something meaningful, Jason?" asked Serena with a huge smile.

"Gawdamn, yes," he whispered, pawing at Alex's hand. "Right, Melissa?"

He lolled his head back at Melissa, who then decided to go to the washroom or something. She disappeared in a cloud of Exclamation! perfume.

"I'm drunk. I'm very, very drunk," he said, sadly wagging his head. "But"—he lifted his hand, pointed a finger at Alex—"not so drunk that I can't ask 'er for a dance. Okay, Alex? 'Kay?" Right in her face.

She wanted to escape. She wanted to leave. To hide.

A hand on her bare shoulder. She turned to see Peter, resplendent in a T-shirt emblazoned with a thunderbird, black tuxedo pants and cummerbund, a black opera cape. He opened up his arms. "Dance with me, darling."

She laughed but felt like crying. She stood, wobbling slightly in her satin heels. He led her onto the dance floor, where he promptly lost all his bravado. He put his head on her shoulder and confessed, "It's this night. I don't know. I felt so good. And now I feel like crap. Know what I mean? Nothing feels real."

The music man started up with "Stairway to Heaven." She swayed with Peter, in one spot, until the lights came on again.

Later, when Serena came back to her place, trailing a peach satin jacket, the morning light beginning to pierce its way past post-graduation-dance fog, they collapsed on Alex's bed, a bag of taco chips between them and a carton of milk that Alex had hauled out of the kitchen downstairs.

"You never tell me what's going on in your head. Not really," said Serena. She had found a half-eaten package of M&M's at the bottom of her purse and socked back a handful, munched thoughtfully, shoved her hand back into the taco bag.

"Why are you telling me this?" said Alex.

"I always have to guess." Serena turned her head on the pillow. "Don't tell me you enjoyed yourself tonight."

Alex remembered the way Peter clung to her on the dance floor. And how Serena, sitting at the table, had watched them, straight shouldered, with an excruciating unveiled longing.

She wished that he were here now, not Serena. To have his lone-wolf heart right here, beating beside her own, that would be comfort enough.

"You're such a good friend to me," continued Serena sadly. "You put up with all my crap. And I always end up disappointing you."

Alex shivered, sank down under her quilt.

"Like I'm looking at you dancing with Peter tonight. And I'm thinking—I don't know what made me think it—but I started thinking about your grandpa. About how he was such a pal. Always around. Like the best dad. Know what I mean? Steady as a rock. You were so lucky to have him—even if it was only for part of your life."

"Don't let's talk about this right now. Okay?" Hot tears began to pool in her eyes. She blinked them away. Reaching over, she took Serena's hand and held on tightly to this friend from her childhood days. She felt as if she were sinking. As if she could disappear altogether. And no one would be able to find her again.

"Alex," said Serena as they both blinked up at the ceiling, "I have to say something. I'm sorry I ran out

on you. You know, with Peter. That I sort of abandoned you. Again. Like, it was all just so stupid. I
don't know if I will ever forgive myself for doing that.
But, you know, and this is the truth, sometimes you
make people feel so lonely."

Two nights later, she had another dream. In this one
she is sitting in front of a large slate-colored rock. It's
drum shaped, about three feet in circumference. She
and Grandpa and Old Raven Man are all around it,
beating it, trying to make its voice come alive. It's a
frightening ceremony. She feels her own voice rise in
song. It comes from a deep and primal place. As the
song rips up toward the sky, the rock begins to pulse
with life. And its life is huge, as if it is waking up from
a century-long sleep. She is awestruck that a rock can
be so alive. She's worried that it will sprout feet and
walk.

Drenched in sweat, she woke up and reeled off the
bed. Staggered to her dresser. Pulled off her nightshirt
and hauled on another one. In bed again, she fell back
into a stunned sleep.

In the morning, she contemplated how her dreams
fell into two categories. There were the ordinary
dreams, like the usual kind people have every night.
And then there were what she'd begun to think of as
the big, scary dreams. The drum dream was another
of those. Lying in the middle of her bed, in the June
sunlight, she still felt its overwhelming spell.

She shivered every time she thought about it, all

day, at her weekend job at Cuppa Java, where she foamed milk and emptied tiny containers of coffee grounds and made an endless procession of lattes and mochas and cappuccinos and vegetarian sandwiches. She thought about it, and goose bumps did a slow loose-minded dance up and down her arms.

Back in her room at night, as she lit a candle, the phone rang. It was Peter. He had something to give her. Could he come over?

Twenty minutes later, he appeared at her back door with a huge unrolled poster of Geena Davis and Susan Sarandon as they appeared, on their road trip, in *Thelma & Louise.*

"You're Thelma," he said, rolling it up, handing it to her. "I've always thought you look sort of like Geena Davis. The red highlights in your hair. The eyes. The bones. This is your graduation gift. It's all I could afford."

"Peter, I didn't buy you anything."

He pulled her against him. Kissed the top of her head. She wanted to tell him how she felt about him. How complicated that was. Maybe he knew already. His arms trembled.

And then he whispered, "You're a wonderful person, Alex. You know that, don't you? You are a queen. A goddess." He held her at arm's length, grinning at her as if she were just too good to be true.

Something caught her eye past his shoulder. She looked out to his car by the curb. The door was open. Some blond guy with bare arms sat, legs stretched out the passenger's side, cigarette in his long fingers. He squinted at them through a trail of smoke, then smiled a beautiful smile. The evening was calm and humid. The cedars in the front yard were heavy with earthy perfume.

She smiled brightly at Peter, didn't know what to say or where to look. And then she did look at him, and he looked back, clear-eyed and solemn, waiting.

Finally she told him, simply, "I hope you have a good time."

He walked away, stopped, turned around. He gave a slow smile and then, right in the middle of the sidewalk, did an ironic little dance all for her.

Later, around one in the morning, still awake, in the dark, staring at the ceiling, she thought about the stunning truth of Peter's life. And then her mother's familiar soft rap came at the door.

"I figured you'd still be up," she said, coming into the room.

Alex rolled over, struck a match, and lit the candle again. She patted the side of her bed for Mom to sit down. Her mother's hair was pulled back with a brilliant yellow silk-wrapped elastic band. She sat down cross-legged on the bed. Her satiny knees poked out from under bold-striped cotton pajamas. She smelled faintly of L'Air du Temps perfume, which she put on every morning even if she only went across the hall to the little bedroom that Grandpa had transformed for her into an office space. Alex remembered his ten-year-old Chevy truck, full of lumber, parked under the cedar trees, the plate on the front that said *I'm Spending My Kids' Inheritance*.

"I want to talk to you about something," said Mom.

"Sure." Alex's heart rose high and achy in her throat.

"I want to offer you my car for the week," Mom began, "to go out to your father's. To Earl's."

"You're offering me your car? For a whole week? Why?"

"The weather is beautiful now, and there's a lake where you could swim. I think it would be good for you. Put back some sparkle." She ran a cool thumb just under Alex's eye along the cheekbone. "If the cabin isn't livable, well, then don't stay. Or if you get there, and you can't face being alone, then just come home."

Alex pulled at the loose threads on her sky blue quilt with the giant tree that always seemed to grow as you drew it up over you. She had always loved this amazing quilt. She loved to lie in the center of her bed, her hands reaching over the covers to stroke the gold-and-green branches. Christmas morning, when she was fourteen, and Mom's eyes were so shiny with delight, and she knew the quilt had been much too expensive, she had said softly, "Cool," and felt guilty, but it had been on her bed ever since.

"Alex," Mom said, "when I fell in love with your father, I never thought about how my life might turn out. I was nineteen years old. I was just a baby. How could I know anything? But I've been lucky in my life. And you're lucky, too. Take your courage into your hands, and don't turn away this gift."

After she left, Alex flicked out the candle. Outside her window, the city night hummed restlessly along. Here, in the darkness of her own room, with her eyes closed tight, her hands stroked the cool raised edges of cotton tree limbs.

13

She is running down the hill, through amber grasses, to the shores of the lake. "Wait for me!" she calls to them. "Look at me. I'm here. I've decided to come. Wait! Oh, please wait!"

"Your granddaughter," Old Raven Man says calmly, pulling a bone-handled jackknife from his pocket. One expert slash, and the fish is split up the middle.

"Hello, Alexandra," Grandpa says.

"Hello, Grandpa. Oh, hello! Hello!" she cries joyfully.

He's hunkered down, whittling a point on a willow stick. She wants him to turn around.

"Look at me, look at me!" she says, just the way she used to at the pool, where he'd sit in the bleachers, her extra towel, her gym bag, and a snack for her beside him.

But he still won't turn around. The jacket he always wore when he took her on camping trips hangs loosely around him. He's as thin as he was when he died.

"Would you like some fish?" Old Raven Man asks. He turns his eyes on her. She is struck by their beautiful light.

"This is your dream," he says, startling her. "You can call me whatever you want. I used to have a name. A long time ago when I was over there. I don't miss it."

He adds wistfully, "I do miss honey. That was good. I remember what it tasted like. Would you like some fish?" he asks a second time.

She should say yes to be polite. But she hates fish, and so she says no.

"It's a spirit fish. They taste like honey." He smiles sweetly at her.

"How are you, Alexandra?" Grandpa asks. He spears the fish with the willow branch and leans it, to cook, over a fire.

She hesitates behind him. She hardly dares to ask, but she has to. "Are you really my grandfather?"

"More or less," he says, turning around. "But of course I've changed."

His eyes, like those of Old Raven Man, are clear and light filled. He is a beautiful spirit. She realizes, suddenly, that she didn't have to worry about him. He's finding his way.

He takes her hand, squeezing it three times like he used to. It was their signal. It meant, I love you.

"I miss you," she says. "Why did you have to go away and leave me?" She starts to cry. Her tears feel real even though she knows that she is only dreaming.

"Why," asks Old Raven Man, "don't you believe your dreams?"

"Because they aren't real," she says, wishing they were, feeling her whole body shudder with tears.

"There isn't anything you can dream that isn't real. Close your eyes," he instructs kindly.

"But I'm dreaming. You're tricking me. This is just a dream. This is just a dream. This is just a dream. . . ."

Grandpa wraps an arm around her. She smells the aftershave he always wore. "You have eyes to see the world with," he explains, "and eyes to see your soul with."

"I'm afraid," she says, "of . . . what I'll find."

"You are afraid of being powerless," says Old Raven Man. She hears him stir the fire. "That's why we're here. We're here to give you power."

She doesn't feel powerful at all. She feels weak and raw. As if she is being pushed to the edge of the world. But she does as she is told. She closes her inner eyes.

"What do you see?" Grandpa asks.

"Darkness," she says, terror rising.

"Let your mind wander. Just let it go." Old Raven Man's soft voice, like clicks of rain.

And so she lets go. She falls. Spiraling down to the unknown. Even as she rushes away, the fishermen appear above her. And she sees, with relief, that she is connected to them by thin strong lines. She turns and tumbles to the edge of the sea of her being. And then she drops even farther. To the deepest place. To where it's no longer dark. A light surrounds her. She is at the warmest, farthest, brightest place within herself.

"A very big light," she says from this deep place. "That's what I see."

"Ah!" Old Raven Man utters a great echoing sigh. "She has found the Great Spirit."

She pulls up, with effort, from Divinity.

Old Raven Man takes the fish from the fire. She can feel the drumming of his heart as he peels away the skin. He offers her a piece of the smoky flesh. She takes it from the rivers of lines on the palm of his hand. As he promised, spirit fish tastes like honey.

part two

THE LEGACY

1

*T*his small blue car pulled into the yard. Pop looked up from his coffee, like a man who had just heard thunder. Lonny stood, still holding his mug, his heart racing.

The girl got out of the car. She was not at all what he expected. A big girl. Big boned, big breasted, loose limbed. Tall as him. With the blackest eyes the color of chokecherries, her fine dark red hair backlit by the morning sun. Amazing and prideful. Queen Bee, he thought, and then felt weak, like someone had just come up behind him and thwacked him hard at the backs of his knees. He tottered unsteadily toward her. "Alexandra?"

"Yes," said the girl, not smiling or flipping her hair or doing any of the cute things that girls he knew did when they flirted with him. "How did you know it was me?" She stared him down with her wild black eyes. She blasted through his veneer, through the walls that he'd so carefully built.

The spirits rushed up from the mound. He could feel their old and powerful reel. They knew, like Pop, that she was coming.

2

*T*he girl sat there, staring out at the LaFrenière homestead. He thought, She's never going to get out of this truck. She had the same expression as her father's the day he took over the land. But with her, it was different. She was a hell of a lot prettier than Earl McKay. Scarier, too.

And this wasn't the way he'd thought it would happen. He'd been prepared to hate her. He'd played over in his mind her moment of arrival, circling back to one image: Pop, once again, in weighted despair over the reminder, thrown back in his face, that his only living heir had rejected this land.

But Pop looked at her, sitting between them, as if she were a delicate package that had just been hand delivered. He then opened his door. He swung his bearlike body down and stood in the tall grasses, eyes lowered, waiting with a kind of huge and noble grace.

It's one of those long hot evenings in August, and he and Mom are sitting on the steps in front of the house. He's telling her that he's had several dreams about bears. In one dream, he's watching TV, eating popcorn, and a bear comes right through the window and curls up on the sofa beside him.

I wasn't even surprised about the bear, he tells her. In my dream it was normal. Well, she says, that bear is telling you something. Bear is a healer. It has powerful medicine. One time, she says, stroking his hair, I had this pain in my heart. It wouldn't go away. Well, I dream that a bear comes and lies down beside me. He stretches his paw way across my chest. I can feel his fur brushing my skin. And he whispers to me. He tells me a love story. And two days later I see that ad your pop put in the paper. And two days after that, he's standing in my doorway, looking like that bear in my dream, and right then and there, I fall in love with him. And the pain in my heart goes away.

Lonny felt a burning pain rise up and lodge itself somewhere near his own heart. And the girl stirred beside him. She drew in a long gentle breath.

Next thing, he was out of the truck. And Pop, furrowing his brow, sent out a silent signal that said: Help her down. But Lonny's hand was already shooting out. She grabbed hold, soft skin, strong hand.

He was still holding on as the spirit passed between them. A woman, he decided. Yes, bent over, weeping, clasping her arms in a keening motion around her own body. As clear as memory, she had passed right through their clasped hands.

He quickly dropped the girl's hand, before she could

notice that his own hands had begun to tremble. They wouldn't stop. He had to fold his arms and hide them under his armpits. Then he realized that she wasn't seeing anything but the pale morning light, spreading itself like pure and god-given honey all over the land that was Earl's legacy to her.

3

"You see now why we couldn't let you drive your little car in here," Mr. LaFrenière was saying. "You can just leave it parked up at our place. It'll be fine there. Your dad never bothered to have a proper road put in. Didn't own a vehicle himself. He'd just show up at our place if he needed a ride to town."

The cabin her father had built was set down in a grove of trees. It was a disappointment. Small, ordinary, undistinguished. The leaves all around sent up a chatter in the light wind. A sad-looking log structure sagged on its last legs to her far left.

Mr. LaFrenière, standing beside the truck, said, "Didn't hardly give you a chance to catch your breath, I guess," and then added shyly, "Rushing you over here like this."

"That's fine," she said. "I was anxious to see the place."

Mom and Auntie Francine, out on the concrete driveway back home, poking their heads through the rolled-down windows, driving her crazy with questions and information: Have you checked the oil, the tires? Do you have your map? Don't go down Highway 3. Take Highway 1 because it's faster and more direct and there's less chance of getting lost. Did you remember your sunglasses? Did you buy that sunscreen? You should take your jacket, the green one with the fleece lining. I don't care if it is June. The nights around a lake can get cold. Now don't you forget to phone us when you get there. Do you have Mr. LaFrenière's address?

Maybe I won't stay, she thought. Maybe I'll just take a look around, get back in their truck, go back to their place. I'll tell them I'm not planning on staying. Just like that. It'll be easy.

"You like it then?" Mr. LaFrenière asked, anxious as a child.

"Yes," she said, pinned to the spot and humbled.

He nodded his big head. Flicked at a couple of bright leaves that were stuck to the truck's fender. "That body of water you see out there is called Fatback Lake. Your dad got to look at it mostly in winter. When I was a boy, I would skate there sometimes."

The lake, rolling away from the slight rise on which the cabin sat, was as familiar to her as her dreams. Cold prickles began to dance up her arms, along her neck, into her scalp. It was, in fact, the lake where she had dreamed about Grandpa and Old Raven Man fishing, where they had flipped a huge radiant creature from the deep dark waters. Where she had floated down and down through darkness into the light inside her soul. Where she had shared with them the honey-tasting flesh of the spirit fish.

She swung around and looked at the hill behind her. A low buzz began to grow in her ears. She tasted the cold memory of snow on her tongue. Black wings flapped powerfully against her chest. And then, as the enchantment grew, a brilliant winter sky, a cabin with windows looking east to the lake, west to the hill.

Without warning, her whole body reacted, became unbalanced. Dizzily she sank down, stretched her legs in front of her, hung her head, inhaled the green early-summer heat.

"You just sit there for a while," Mr. LaFrenière said kindly. "It will take some getting used to."

Think about something else. No, not the boy, standing there with his arms folded. His gorgeous black shiny hair. The smell of sage rising around him.

Mr. LaFrenière went on, "This is undeveloped land that's been in my family for a hundred years. When your dad bought it, he promised me that he wouldn't change it except to build his cabin over there. He kept his promise."

She breathed deeply. "Mr. LaFrenière," she said. "I've never even seen a photograph of my father. What did he look like?" And then she added, "When you knew him."

"He was a tall man. A little taller than you." He took off his cap, running a massive hand like a bear paw through his hair, then offered, "And, I think, he was a tired man."

He was a tired man. A tired man.

"How long are you staying?" the boy, Lonny, suddenly asked.

"My mom lent me her car for the week," she said, her guts churning. Please don't let me throw up on this grass, right in front of him.

"You won't be using it much." He scanned some faraway green place across the lake. His eyes were unreadable.

She struggled back to her feet.

They unloaded her things from the back of the truck and set them on the wooden front steps of her father's cabin: boxes of food supplies that her mother had carefully packed, two coolers, a big army kit bag, and three plastic bags full of every conceivable necessity—pillows, sheets, her cotton tree quilt, a first-aid kit, extra shoes, three thick wool sweaters, a flashlight, and so on.

"If you need anything, there's a phone," said Mr. LaFrenière. "That dad of yours wasn't altogether against modern equipment. I guess you knew that your mother called a couple of weeks back to say you'd be around sometime this summer." He smiled and added, "So everything works. Everything's in order. And by the way, the water's okay, but it doesn't taste so good. We haul our drinking water from town." He looked at Lonny. "So we'll leave now and let her get settled in. You can bring a jug of water down to her later. You'll do that, won't you, son."

It isn't too late. Say something. They're leaving. God, don't leave me here.

Lonny turned away. She watched him stride quickly

over to the truck. Like he could hardly wait to get in and leave. He jumped inside and slammed the door shut and leaned against the steering wheel.

Mr. LaFrenière pulled some keys out of his pocket. Two bright brass keys on a dull beaded brass chain. "He's got something eating at him today," he said apologetically. "These are the keys—one for the cabin, the other for the shed out back. And the power box is inside the kitchen. Main switch is right by the door. Just flip it on." He paused, as if he was forgetting something, then said, "Would you like some help inside with your things?"

He had warm brown eyes and a courtly manner. She half expected him to tip his cap.

"I can manage," she said.

"Well, then, welcome to your little home, miss."

"Mr. LaFrenière?" she blurted out.

"Yes?"

"I'll be fine."

With a little nod, he said, "Call us anytime. Our number is posted on the wall beside the phone."

He walked slowly back to the truck. He heaved himself into the passenger's side. Heavily closed the door.

Lonny lifted an arm over the seat and, looking over his shoulder, backed up the truck with a careless grace that took her breath away. Then he stopped and slowly moved ahead, bumping up the long trail back to the prairie road. For a while, she could hear him shifting gears. The engine's slightly asthmatic whine. And then she was alone.

4

The truck jouncing back up the trail. A thin bead of sunlight breaking through the poplars, shining in his eyes. Pop giving him the third degree. Why was he "so rude to her"? And "Why every time you have to go into that property do you act that way?"

"What way?"

"You know." Pop looked hurt. He rubbed his hand over his chin. Let that big hand fall helplessly onto his lap and then drummed his knee with his fingers.

"No. I don't know."

But of course he knew. And then they didn't speak to each other the rest of the way. And when they got there, he offered to go to town and pick up the mail and whatever else they needed. Maybe go and see Deena at the deli, pick up some hamburgers and her thick crispy french fries. He'd buy a can of creamed corn, Pop's favorite.

Pop just took off his cap, slapped it against his trouser leg, and put it on again. He squinted forlornly at a gray cloud.

"Dammit, Pop, say something."

Didn't say anything. Shook his head and wandered off in the direction of the workshop. So now he'd be in there until all hours, tinkering with stuff. Fixing things that didn't need to be fixed.

The way she sank down in the grass at Earl's place, he thought maybe he was wrong. Maybe she did see it. It, whatever it was. The way she hung her head, sickly, over her knees. That little bone at the back of her neck sticking up. Something was happening, that was for sure. And it was scaring the shit out of him, attracted to this girl who conjured up his childhood terrors as easily as breathing.

5

A thin trail of her father's life was scattered throughout the cabin. But it was nothing out of the ordinary. In the bathroom, the shower head leaked and drizzled rust-colored water. So she unscrewed it and fixed it. Of course that then led to the floors, which she scrubbed with the rusty water and the only soap she could find, a half-used bottle of dandruff shampoo. But the rest of the place still smelled of old grease. Did he fry everything? And there were little dried-up pools, everywhere, of candle wax.

Before she changed it, the calendar on the wall by the phone still said *January*. On a hook behind the bedroom door, she found a bent-up cowboy hat hanging over a well-worn brown leather jacket with a fur collar, and under that a pair of misshapen brown corduroy pants and a green wool cardigan sweater with two pockets. She picked everything up and carefully went through every pocket. Made a small inventory of what she found: a paper clip, five dusty acorns, a smooth white stone with maroon markings, four toothpicks, a small red-handled jack-knife.

She piled the clothing beside the living-room door. A door that opened onto nothing. No landing. No steps. Straight down, three feet, onto wild prairie grass.

Her father and, she supposed, the LaFrenières before him had simply allowed all that green and mauve and amber grass, strewn with little white wild-flowers, to roll away, down the sloping embankment onto the rocky shores of the lake. She sat there, gazing out over the ruffled water until the breeze died and the mosquitoes started to urge themselves into the cabin.

Then she tried calling home. Remembered that Mom, whom she should have called earlier, was going shopping with Auntie Francine and then to dinner and a late movie, so that they wouldn't worry about her, which they probably were doing anyway. So she left a message on the machine: "Hi, Mom. Hi, Auntie Francine. It's me. It's Alex. I'm here. I didn't get lost. I'm fine. Mom, I'll call you later. Or I'll call tomorrow. Or something."

She got off the phone and called Peter. His little brother, Dougy, answered with a bored voice and didn't want to talk to her, and in the background she could hear the TV turned way up and some girl who was with him singing in a weird voice like she was part duck.

"So will you give him the message?"

"Yeah. Sure."

"Dougy, did you even write down the number? Read it back to me."

"I've *got* it! Bye."

She knew that Peter wouldn't get her message. She put down the phone. The LaFrenières' phone number was right there in her father's familiar scrawly hand. She stroked her fingers over it, feeling the ridges and hollows the pressure of his pen had made. *555–3651, Tom and Lonny LaF.*

The sun was just slanting, late-day gold grazing the top of the big hill behind the cabin. She hadn't eaten since late morning, two doughnuts before she drove onto their property, just before they brought her here. The clock over the fridge had stopped working who knows how long ago, at seven minutes to three. Besides the clock, the kitchen contained a woodstove, a table, one chair, and the refrigerator. A sofa, a little table, and a circular braided rug were in the living room. A bed and an empty bureau in the bedroom. That was it. No pictures. No ornaments. No really personal traces other than the clothing.

Oh, and in the kitchen, a few pots, dishes, utensils. And in one kitchen drawer, wrapped carefully in dark pink tissue paper, she found seven fat white candles and a perfect round, low candleholder. Green, green stone. Dark and smooth. Beautiful. She cradled the candleholder in the palm of her hand and went and lay down on the bed. She sprawled on her back. She placed the green stone on her abdomen, breathing deeply, feeling its weight. Letting it gently rise and fall, rise and fall. She tried to relax. She tried to sleep. Then she stared at the ceiling and tried to feel at home.

6

After the sun, a great fiery ball, started to edge the rim of the prairies, he went out and watched a hawk fly with ponderous dignity off a fence post, walked over the sagging wires and silvery wolf willow onto what was now Jacob Wiebe's pastureland.

He came to a circle of white rocks and looked down at a dried cow pie. Prairie grass grew right up through it, and it crumbled under a light kick. He thought about how many buffalo had once grazed here. How many of their bones were scattered or crumbled or buried. How many generations of pasture sage had grown up from this very earth they had walked on, from their bones and dust and blood and hearts.

All these thoughts became jumbled with images of the dark-eyed girl over at Earl's place. The white sleeve of her T-shirt resting against her smooth arm. Her lofty nose. The smell of her, sitting between him and Pop, as they drove over there in the truck. Damn, she smelled good. Like clover or something. How did she get that smell? It didn't come from a perfume bottle.

It came from her. It drove him nuts, the memory of that sweet smell.

The sky was turning a pale smoky blue when he got back. He hadn't bothered with eating, hadn't been hungry. Hollow as old bones, and light-headed, he stood by the refrigerator door, slowly drinking cold town water out of a plastic juice jug.

Earlier, he'd watched Pop eat two of Deena's burgers, two bags of fries, a side order of onion rings, and a bowl of creamed corn speckled with Cajun pepper, his eyes lowered the whole time over his food. And now he was back in the workshop. Lonny could see his light from the kitchen window.

The telephone rang, and it was Robert. Dunderhead had run off again. "Damn him," said Robert. "You can never count on that stupid dog staying in one spot for ten minutes. Have you seen him?" Lonny said that he hadn't, and then Robert stayed on the line for several minutes more talking about Tammy, who always had her nose in the air now that she was going out with Richard Dobson, whom everybody knew would end up a lawyer just like his father.

Lonny interrupted his friend in midsentence, midstream. "Robert, go out and find yourself somebody else."

Silence. And, "You think?" And then, just like that, he's talking about going up to northern Ontario on a fishing trip with his dad and Uncle Daryl. "Crops are in, and it's a good time to go. *Huge* friggin' muskies, Daryl says. Real fighters, too. You should come with us, Lon. It'd be great."

That day, coming back from the mound after Robert
has pedaled furiously home, he comes into the kitchen.
His mother is there with her back to him. At the sink,
snapping green beans. Snap, in half. Accusingly, into
the waiting bowl.

She says, not turning around, "You see dragonflies
up there all the time. They move around like little
angels. How many did you see today, my babe?"

"I didn't see any." A sick wave of heat rises up his
body.

A west wind whispers against the moth-white kitchen
curtains, blows them in, sighs through her hair.

I've really got to go now, he told Robert, who had
moved on to talking about the ball game he was
pitching over at Poplar Bluff tomorrow night. I'll be
there, Lonny said, even though he had no intention
of going. And after that, Robert finally got off the
phone.

Earl's daughter was waiting for the jug of drinking
water that had been promised to her, and he couldn't
leave it any longer. He filled up a big blue container,
threw it into the truck, and then quickly left, wheels
grinding over gravel, spinning out their bad-luck song.

But three minutes down the road, in the ten-o'clock
twilight, here came Robert's big black Lab, Dunderhead, loping toward him, a red moon rising at his
back. He had a sideways gait and a look of purposeful
attention.

Lonny slowed the truck to a stop, reached over,
and opened the cab door. Dunderhead, panting, pink

tongue lolling, a string of drool whipped over and around his long black nose, gave him a happy look of recognition and began to scramble up into the cab. Lonny had to help him by grabbing the scruff of his neck and giving him an extra boost.

As Lonny closed the door, Dunder licked his face. Then he settled down just like any other passenger going for a ride, eyes facing out the front window.

"Where have you been, Dunder?" said Lonny, pulling back onto the road. "Have you been out chasing tail again?" He put his arm around the dog, who continued to pant and drip drool on the seat.

"Guess I'd better drive you on home then."

Robert's farm was a ten-minute drive in the opposite direction of the LaFrenière homestead. The dog had actually been heading home, but who knows what else might grab his attention and veer him off on a new adventure before he got there.

He remembered back to the year Robert got Dunder, bringing the puppy over in that old blue Snugli that had been used for his little cousin, Daryl Junior. He drove into their yard on his bike, that puppy bouncing against his chest.

Lonny's mom pulled Dunder out of the Snugli and held him and arched her neck back at Pop and said, "We should have one of these."

"I'll get you a dozen, if you like," Pop told her, smiling.

That was the summer she died. They never got a dog. But Dunder had somehow always felt like his own.

"So here's the deal, buddy," Lonny said to the dog's

silky ear. "I've got a mess going on in my life. You believe in spirits? I sure as hell do. Something's after me, you know that? Well, you're a dog. Do dogs ever have a guilty conscience? Do you sleep well at night, boy?"

Dunder stumbled around in three circles on the seat and finally lay down with his head on Lonny's leg.

"I've got some memories," said Lonny, stroking him, "that won't leave me alone. Chase me around in circles. I'm going to tell you something, buddy, that I've never told another living soul. The day that Robert and I dug up the mound, that very night, Mom came into my room. And she sat on the edge of my bed. And she looked at me for a while. Anyway, I'm lying there staring up at the ceiling, not knowing what to do. I felt so terrible. And then Mom says, like she's just guessed or maybe she's known it all day, 'Don't ever tell your pop what you did. It would kill him. That land and that sacred mound mean the world to him. Better he just simply doesn't know. Did you clean it up?'

"I look into her eyes and I tell her yes, and honest to God, Dunder, I don't think I've ever seen such a look from her, a look for me, for her son. I'll never, ever forget that look."

The yard light at Robert's farm shone out in the rose and blue nightfall shadows. Robert came out of the house to greet them.

"Found him on the road," said Lonny.

"Didn't have to bring him around, but thanks anyway," said Robert, opening the passenger's door.

"I was on my way somewhere," said Lonny as Dunder hopped down and rushed toward the house, wagging his tail.

"Come on in for a while anyway. Uncle Daryl's friend Joe Dakotah just stopped by. He's into all kinds of old-time Indian stuff. Uncle Daryl was at a sweat lodge he runs. Last weekend. He's cleaned up his act, Lon, he really has."

He said all this while kicking at the ground with his shoe. Robert's uncle had spent time in jail for growing a crop that wasn't exactly legal, right in the middle of his sunflower field. Everybody in the valley knew about Daryl Lang. They started calling Daryl's field the Drugstore. And when he'd finished serving time, he'd come back, smiling his big piano-keyboard smile. That was over two years ago. Except for the drinking, he had mostly behaved himself ever since. But people had a long memory for things like that.

And Robert really loved Daryl, but no matter how much he tried to convince himself that his uncle had actually reformed, everybody knows how easy it is to fall back into old ways. And Daryl was one of those people who always sat at the edge of the law, even in his good times.

"So come on in," said Robert, urging Lonny with a nod toward the house. "Come on and meet this guy."

Lonny hesitated. "I promised somebody something."

"Can't it wait? I really think you should meet Joe. I really think you'd get a lot out of it."

Robert seldom talked this way, so urgent and pleading. So what'll it hurt? thought Lonny. It's already late, and she's probably given up on me by now anyway.

Dunder was waiting by the door, furiously wagging his tail, and nosed on through the second Robert started to open it. He dashed over to his water dish and drank thirstily, slopping water up over the sides.

Sitting around the kitchen table were Robert's dad and mom and Uncle Daryl and his live-in girlfriend, Louise, and this strange-looking Indian guy, about sixty years old, with a pockmarked face and hair as long as Lonny's all tied back with a black band.

The guy was so Native, so in-your-face, like he was announcing the fact. And it made Lonny feel uncomfortable.

Then the stranger raised his eyes, and for the second time since that morning, since Earl McKay's daughter had stepped out of her car and looked through his soul with her chokecherry-colored eyes, Lonny felt as if his whole life had just been handed over for inspection. Only this guy made him feel like he was a fly on a map, pierced with a pin.

Just a moment was all it took, and then he went on talking as if Lonny hadn't even entered the room. The guy in some strange way was holding court with Robert's family; they were hanging on to his every word with rapt and respectful attention.

Robert's mom stuck out her arm to Lonny, still not taking her eyes off their guest. She was always warm in a matter-of-fact kind of way. He walked over to her, and she pulled out a chair for him to join them.

The guy was talking about how there was a fire in each of us. About how it was sacred. It should never be fanned with alcohol, or it would burn out of control. He didn't look at Robert's uncle Daryl when he said this, but it was a remark that must really have hit home.

Daryl, however, looked soberly down at his hands, then smiled and lifted one hand to stroke Louise's back. He seemed calm. Calmer, in fact, than Lonny could ever remember seeing him.

"Thanks, Joe," Daryl said softly after a moment's silence. "Thanks for stopping by."

"Not a problem." The guy got up and pulled a set of car keys out of his pocket. They were on a metal ring with a buffalo head boldly etched in relief on the silver tag.

Lonny closed his eyes, and beads of perspiration began to break out on his forehead.

"We're holding a doctoring sweat this Sunday afternoon. Two o'clock," said Joe Dakotah.

"I'll be there, Joe," Lonny heard Daryl say, and those words spun out and hit him right in the center of his heart.

"Surprised, him showing up here just like that," Robert's dad said to Daryl after Joe Dakotah got into his car and drove off. He added, with a soft chuckle, "Didn't know he made house calls."

7

They sit side by side in a hot, dark womblike place. Stones as red-hot as lava have been brought in and set down in a pit at the center. A graceful woman in a red nightgown places a small piece of cedar on one stone. It leaves a black pattern, a fossil on fire.

Old Raven Man ladles water over the rocks. They hiss and sing. Heat blisters up.

"Hold your towel over your face," instructs Grandpa.

She does and still smells fire and cedar and another, more acrid smell. Old Raven Man begins to chant and pray. In the scorching darkness she hears something, like little comets, whizzing around and around over their heads. And then something feathery graces her skin, brushing across her bare feet, her arms, her forehead.

Two headlights shone like moons, bouncing across the bedroom wall, flashing across her eyes, waking her up. She had fallen asleep on the hard bed. She had

had many vivid, exhausting dreams. In one, she had chased after her father. She ran through the woods, reaching to touch arms and legs that disappeared into tree limbs, shoulders into mounds of moss, a curved back into the gnarled hardness of stone.

A light knock at the screen door pulled her from this deep place. Slipped her groggily through the mists of sleep and off the bed. She stumbled on bare feet and got to the kitchen.

Beyond the screen a small cobwebby porch light attracted white flying things. Beyond that, the boy, Lonny, waited for her to let him inside.

She snapped on the kitchen light, blinking in its cruel brightness, then opened the door.

He looked at her, and his eyes widened. Then he pushed past. He carried a large blue plastic jug. He set it on the table, then just stood there looking at her.

"Your drinking water," he said finally.

"Oh," she said.

His hair was shiny. He smelled of a light aftershave or cologne that made her think of lilies on water. She wondered what other girls thought of him. Probably they acted like idiots. They likely fell all over themselves. Well, she wasn't going to. What did he mean by coming around so late? He had the kind of sleek, silky spell that made you want to look at your feet. She stared at him hard. She lifted her head and stared at him with her most ferocious concentration.

He said at last, "Probably you should run the taps

for a while. In the kitchen. In the bathroom. The water will improve a little."

"I did that already." She looked at her watch. It was ten past midnight. She added pointedly, "About ten hours ago."

"Ah, good," he said sheepishly. He wore a black shirt over his faded jeans. And cowboy boots.

"So I guess that's it," he said.

"Yes, it is," she said, slipping her gaze to his hands. He had wonderful hands.

He turned to go. She stood at the door. He didn't make her feel too big. They were the same height. He was solidly built.

"It's quiet here," she said, still pissed off, yet wanting him to stay. The screen door creaked slightly. She followed him out to the steps.

"I should get going." He dug his hands into his pockets, hurried down the steps, turned around. "You'll be okay?"

"I'll be fine," she said.

He stared at the ground. Then back at her. And for three seconds held her with his eyes. He rocked slightly, unsteadily, on his feet. Took a couple of steps backward. "I'll check back on you tomorrow," he said, and then hurried to the truck.

Her arm sliding up the door frame, her head mournfully resting against her shoulder, she replied, to his back, "You don't have to do that. Check up on me. I don't need anything. Nothing at all."

He closed the cab door and sat there looking at her

over the steering wheel. She didn't know why she felt like crying. The wind in the trees was lonely. A hollow sound in the moonlight. In the dark behind her father's cabin, the waves crept slowly over the rocks.

She went back inside. Turned off the kitchen light. Walked into the bedroom and stared at the shadowy bed. She swept the stone candleholder off the mattress and went back out to the kitchen.

In a green garbage bag with a plastic tie was her cotton tree quilt. She pulled it out, hugged it against her, inhaling the smells of home. She would sleep on the tacky lime-and-brown paisley sofa in the living room. How could she sleep all night on her dead father's bed? She pulled her tree quilt around her shoulders and looked past the kitchen window.

He was still out there. Sitting in the dark in his truck. She sat down on the kitchen chair, tried to quiet her mind. Listened for the truck to start. Stood up again. Shadowed one shoulder against the window. His head was leaned back on the seat. Was he sleeping? Was something wrong with him? Should she go out?

She trailed her quilt back to the kitchen chair, sat down, thought some more. She didn't know him. Maybe she should lock the doors. She got up, closed the kitchen door as unsuspiciously as possible, locked it. Stole into the living room, locked that door. Eased down on the couch. Sat there, thinking, her eyes closed.

She kept listening for the truck to start up again. It didn't. She wanted to turn on a light. But he'd notice. Wanted to light one of those candles wrapped in the pink paper. There were matches in the cardboard box. She got up and lurched back to the kitchen. Tripped over one of her coolers. Fell hard on the floor. Banged both knees.

Now she was angry. It was her own damn cabin. So why did she have to creep around in it? And why didn't he just take the hell off home? But she didn't want to confront him. She didn't know a thing about him.

She edged back into the living room. Wrapped herself up, cocooned herself in, anchored herself down. Listened to the wind whirling around the house. Listened to the lake. Listened for things in the night. But all she heard was water and wind, and wind and water, and water and wind.

*W*hite stars twinkled in the sky, and white moths threw themselves against the pale bare light over her door. Near the silvery wind-ruffled lake, small frogs croaked and jumped, their gold-fire eyes lit by the moon.

Something powerful, like a finger pointing, had come and jabbed Lonny hard in the middle of his chest, nearly buckling his legs under him. He'd managed to hold his balance and had muttered, "I'll check back on you tomorrow," then turned and quickly left.

Now back in the truck, it was all he could do, his shaking hands on the steering wheel, to keep from starting the engine, throwing it into reverse, and escaping. He could still feel that cold pressure on his skin. It was his mind playing tricks again. Had to be. He was just spooked, that's all. Out here, so exposed, in the darkness.

He took a deep breath for courage and held it, watching this big-boned, long-boned regal girl framed by her father's doorway. She didn't seem anything like him, nothing like Earl. Good thing she'd never had the chance to meet him, to know what an old drunk her father was. Worse than Robert's uncle Daryl on a bad day, especially that last month of his life.

Closing his eyes, he rubbed his hand over his chest and thought that if he could just make it to morning, everything would be fine. But then Joe Dakotah's key chain, the silver metal, the buffalo head, swung abruptly across his mind's eye. Instantly, he knew that everything wasn't fine. That things would not be fine again until he could somehow make them that way. If anything happened to this girl, on this land, it would be on his head. He opened his eyes in time to watch her slip back inside the cabin. The door slowly closed. He would have to stay. What other choice did he have? But what would she think of him, parked outside her door like some crazy haunted animal?

He had to stay through this goddamn night and take care of her and watch over her. There was something out there in the darkness. A presence. Maybe it was the land itself. Telling him that he was not welcome.

He concentrated on her, inside the cabin. What did she look like when she slept? Did she sleep on her side or her stomach? He thought about the back of her neck. The small protruding bone. He thought about her breasts. Then he tried not to think about her breasts. They were beautiful. And big. He shivered. And curled up on the seat. And fell asleep thinking about them.

Toward morning the eastern sun rose up over the

lake right beyond his window. Closing his eyes more tightly, he watched the rosy ball of light behind his inner eye elongate, slowly turn a perfect shape. A buffalo head. Same shape and size as the one on Joe Dakotah's key ring. Something small and hard, like a smooth round pebble, shifted inside his chest, and he felt stronger.

After that he went home. He called his boss at Petro-Can. Told him that he wouldn't be in for a few days. He was going to lie about the reason, but Johnson jumped ahead of him.

"Got things to do, eh?" said Mr. Johnson. "Well, I understand. Heard you did real well at your final year. Your stepdad's been bragging about you again. What are your plans?"

Lonny thought about Earl's last letter to his daughter, remembered how it still lay at the bottom of his bedroom drawer, under a layer of things—an old plastic comb, his eyeglasses that he hadn't worn in several months because of vanity, two packages of unused guitar strings, a book he'd been meaning to read, the ticket stubs from the Tragically Hip concert that he and Robert and Jen Nightingale drove all the way into Winnipeg to see, a year ago this April.

Also, there was the photo of Mom and Deena and him. It had been taken by Pop the year before Mom died. They were standing on top of Medicine Bluff. Mom and Deena had just been tickling him. It had been, he now recalled, a dazzling sunny day. They were framed by blue sky. They were all laughing with their mouths open. It was a memory that made time stand still.

He would have to give this girl her letter. It was something he knew he needed to do, a matter of resolve that lay like a small and sickly thing right at the outer edges of his inner vision. But how could he just hand it to her?

"Mr. Johnson," he said shakily, "I've got some things I've needed to take care of for a long time. That's why I need a few days."

The truth surprised him. So did Johnson's response, although it shouldn't have. He was a good boss. Kind, friendly, always ready to bend over backward with the work schedules.

"Take all the time you need," he said. "I can get Keith or Dan or Jen to fill in for you. It's hard, these days, for young people to figure out where they're going. See you," he said, adding cheerfully, "whenever."

Lonny grabbed a quick shower and left Pop still asleep. Lately, on his days off, he'd been sleeping in more than usual. Then he pulled out Earl's letter and took it out to the truck. He threw it in the glove compartment and drove back through the fresh morning air to see her.

9

$\mathcal{T}$he wind had died just before dawn, and cradled in a balloon of silence, she had woken up briefly and then fallen back to sleep. When she woke again, the sun was fully up. Birds sang outside the window screens. She wondered if he was still out there and staggered to her feet and went to the kitchen window.

Where his truck had been, tire marks made pathways like memories in the long green-and-golden grass.

She felt a trickle of relief. Then disappointment. Then an overwhelming hollow loneliness. She went over to the kitchen wall and picked up the phone. The only person in the world she wanted to talk to now was Mom. Even if it meant waking her up.

On the second ring her mother picked up the phone. "You're okay? You got there all right? No trouble with the car?"

"I'm fine, Mom. Everything's fine."

"Everything works?"

"Yes. It's a very small cabin, but everything works."

The city seemed so far away. How could it be that she had been there only twenty-four hours ago? Something about this place, the way it caught you in its spell, made time seem to stretch. It tricked you. It made you think that *this* was real time: wind time. Leaf time. Grass time. Lake time. Pulse-of-the-earth time.

"I'm glad you left your message on the machine," her mother was saying, "because then I knew Mr. LaFrenière had taken care of the phone just like I'd asked him to, and here you are." She hurried on. "So do you like it, this land that Earl . . . your dad left you?"

Alex could hear the little catch in her voice and didn't know what to do with all the guilt that that made her feel. Maybe she should invite her to come out here. Francine could bring them both in her car. No, she thought, I have to get used to being here first. I have to do this on my own without Mom and Auntie Francine loving me to death and driving me nuts with all their good intentions.

"It must be very green there," Mom continued, sounding very far away.

She breathed deeply, once. Closed her eyes. There were things swimming in the lake. She could vividly see them. Could see movement through deep green. Could see their eyes looking at her.

"Is it a big lake? It looks quite small on the map. But it must be good for swimming—"

"Mom," Alex interrupted, "I'm feeling a bit foggy.

I haven't eaten in a while. Is it okay if I go and have some breakfast?"

"That's fine," said Mom, sounding hurt and cut off, "I shouldn't be bothering you. I just wanted to know that you were . . . settled."

"Mom, it's okay. I called *you*, remember? You're not bothering me. Really. It's just all . . . a little over-whelming."

And now I'm going to cry, she thought, and make her worry, when all I wanted to do was be a strong person.

"Alex?"

She swallowed the damn lump. She set her shoulders. I will not cry, she thought, and then she said, "Yes, I'm still here, Mom."

"I'm sorry if I'm upsetting you. Try to have a good time. Francine says to tell you that if the loneliness gets too intolerable, you can always come home. Nobody will think the worse of you. You know that, don't you?"

"I know that, Mom. Thank Francine for me any-way. Thank her for the thought."

"Alex, you sound very funny. You sound very far away."

"Mom. I'm okay. Really."

"Well . . . please take care of yourself."

"I will. I wish you wouldn't worry about me."

She got off the phone and began to pull milk and orange juice and cheese and eggs out of her father's once-empty fridge. Then she felt nauseated. She put them all back again. Next, she hauled out a loaf of twelve-grain. She opened the plastic bag, ripped off a corner of bread, looked at it in her hand, thought about eating it, and stuffed it back in the bag.

In the bathroom, she turned on the water taps. Watched the water slowly turn a slightly different color. Not perfect. But better. Peeling down, she got into the shower and stood there for a long time, letting the steamy water beat down on her body. She opened her mouth. The water had a metallic taste. And it was slightly salty. She wondered if it was a taste you could get used to. She stood there for the longest time. Thought about the fact that this water wasn't treated, like city water. It just came up, as it was, from deep in the ground.

After, she pulled on jeans and a T-shirt and socks and boots and went outside, her hair still dripping. Made her way slowly across grasses, their tops flattened by winds. Always winds here. Even when they lowered to a whisper, you could still feel their breath on your skin.

She walked toward the hill and thought about what Mr. LaFrenière had said yesterday about her father: He was a tired man. Then she tried to picture him but failed. A tall gray form with fuzzy edges. A tired man. So why does a tired man buy up all this property in the middle of nowhere, and then hide himself away in a cabin? Did he have strange dreams, too? Did he have waking visions? Did Grandpa come to him in the middle of the night?

She pictured Grandpa's silver spirit hovering a few inches off the floorboards. "Earl," he whispers to the lump who is quaking with fear under an old thin blanket, "why did you tease her with those puny letters? You made her want to have a real father. You made her think half her life was missing. Well, it's time to do something about it. Show yourself." Grandpa reaches out and grabs a tattered end of the withered blanket. He whips it off the bed. Abracadabra, nobody's there.

She turned and quickly walked ahead, legs swishing though a tangle of grasses. She pushed ahead, on up the hill through bush where cobwebs hung, thinly beaded with dew, and thought about Grandpa and Old Raven Man instead. She pulled them close against her inner mind. She felt the comfort of these two old men, walking beside her. They urged her along. Grandpa's red Tansi Lumber cap pulled down over his eyes. Old Raven Man's gentle head, white hair flowing in the wind along the collar of that oh-so-familiar black wool coat. Three buttonholes. One button, the middle one, missing. The other two shiny as a bird's eyes.

Up through deep fragrance—leaf and root and moss. Up to the place where trees rustled. Up past those trees to full sunlight. To the treeless, grassy, mounded top. And there to sink down.

Look around the rim of the prairie land. See what others have seen for thousands of years. Turn your eyes skyward now, to where a small cloud, like a puff of smoke, is making its way to the heavens.

10

*H*e found her up there on the mound, lying back in the grass. Her long hair fanning out from her skull. Her eyes closed. He knew she would be exactly where he and Pop had sat that first day, when he was seven years old, and the world was a lot less complicated.

He didn't want to startle her. Lowering himself quietly, he sat on his heels and waited.

Her lashes fluttered. With a little gasp, she sat up.

For one fearful second he thought she would run. Or that he would. But neither of them did. He exhaled slowly.

"Where did you come from?" she said, looking all around her.

"Dropped like a hawk out of the sky," said Lonny with a nervous smile. I'll bet she can see the corners of my mouth twitching, he thought. I'll bet this little old girl sees right through me and all my romantic bullshit.

She had pulled off her boots and socks. He looked sidelong at her feet. They were small and pretty and out of proportion with the rest of her.

"I was here all night," he said, rubbing the back of his neck, surprised at himself for saying such a thing out loud.

"I know." She curved back her head, looking curiously at him with those eyes. It was such a look, seeming to enter his soul, dart around, search for a light.

He slid his gaze away and said, "I fell asleep. That's what happened. And then I took off early this morning." He pulled up a stalk of grass so he would have something to do with his hands. He plunged ahead. "Did you sleep okay?"

"Yes."

"It gets very dark out here at night."

"I noticed that."

"I thought you might be scared your first night here."

"I wasn't."

There was pride in her voice. She's lying, he thought. She was probably scared to death, sleeping all alone in dead Earl's cabin. Looking at his feet, at the cabin down the hill, at the lake, at anything but her, he said, "I used to come up here a lot, but things changed. Life. Stuff like that."

He finally looked at her again and smiled, and smelled her sweet smell, and felt a raw and burning ache slowly rise up his body.

She had a delicate mouth. But she didn't smile back. "So. You and your dad live alone?"

"He's actually my stepdad. My mom died a long time ago."

"Oh. I'm sorry," she said with real sympathy.

"Pop and I get along pretty good."

Her hands were now flat out behind her. She rested on them. Beneath her hands, beneath the earth, who knew what lay there.

"Did you know my dad very well?" She turned her head, her wild eyes, to look him full in the face.

"Not really." His heart began to pump erratically. "We didn't see him that much. He stuck to himself."

"I never got to meet him, my dad," she said, looking away down the long grassy slopes.

Lonny thought about Earl. About the last time he'd seen him alive, the tuneless whistle that had lingered long after the man himself had disappeared into the late afternoon in January. I have to tell her, he thought, I have to tell her about the LaFrenière land. About how unwelcoming it can be. About how my carelessness made it this way.

"A lot of people have died here," he said, and almost stopped, because it sounded naked and awful all out in the open like that. "This . . . where we're sitting," he continued, "is called Medicine Bluff. It was, is, a burial mound."

The breeze clattered through the poplar leaves and in shuddering whispers swept up and away. He pushed past the coldness that prickled at his skin. Squinted instead at the hot sun. Told her about Pop and him coming up here. Pop's theory. The day he and Robert found the skull. How they flew with it back to Pop and Mom.

He stopped right there. "I have to tell you this," he explained. "I have to tell it to you because it's important for you to know."

She sat, quietly composed. But she leaned in on him a little and looked straight ahead as if she were glimpsing some oncoming thing and didn't know if it would be a blessing or a disaster. And he got right back to telling this perfect stranger his terrible story.

He reached the part about the spade, coming back here . . . right down the side of the hill . . . there, at that spot where the grasses and wildflowers look the same as they did seven years ago . . . before they dug in there.

He pushed away his feelings about what he and Robert had done. Giving her the facts. He got to the part where the bigger skeleton started to emerge and kept right on telling it, the arrowhead, the necklace, those human ribs . . . and he stopped. His skin felt colder still under the morning sunlight. He felt he should continue; he'd come this far. Felt as overwhelmed with nausea as he had that day. Felt like an eleven-year-old kid again.

Then she did the oddest thing. She took his hand, cupped it between both of hers. He wanted to pull away. She hung on. She wouldn't let him go. He thought about his mother's cool fingers. Thought about her last dance with Pop. Thought that he couldn't handle any more of this.

"That's it. That's all there is to tell," he said, feeling shame and fear and sadness wash at his heart in waves. "We buried it again. And the skull of the baby, or little kid, or whatever it was. And then we left."

She was still holding on to his hand. Maybe she was doing this to comfort him. The way somebody might come along and comfort a pathetic person they see crying at a bus station. He pulled his hand away.

11

When he'd appeared beside her, hunkered down in the grass, he'd seemed as if he was part of the hill. As if he had just sprung up out of it.

She caught her breath out of the quiet and peaceful ordinariness of this one thing. Of seeing him suddenly there. Of seeing his pale jeans, his T-shirt, his boots with the little traces of scuffed silver on the toes and on the heels. The smell of his wet hair under the sun. The smell of the plants around them and of the warm earth. The smell of her own skin.

And then his confession, spun out so close, she could sometimes feel his breath in her ear. She was starting to be aware of something else, too, a kind of vibration, a very dull drumming. Felt more than heard, it came from right beneath them, from right inside the earth. It grew. It heightened every single word he said.

It was when Lonny stopped his confession, pulling away his hand, that she realized there was something else he wasn't able to tell her. Some heavy sadness.

She recognized its density. Felt it in her arms and legs. "It's hard for you to be here," she said at last.

His head practically hung over his feet.

"Kids do stuff. Probably anybody might have done the same thing."

He said, into his boots, *"Probably?"*

"I'm not excusing it."

He raised his head, didn't look at her, his profile framed by tall grass, little bushes.

"I dreamed that my dad died," she told him, and it came out as naturally as taking her next breath. "My grandpa, who was already dead, and another spirit came to me . . . in dreams. They were here. On this land. It was winter. Deep snow everywhere. That lake was frozen solid as rock. I've never been here before, but I know this place. I know it."

And now she really could feel them behind her, whispering. Grandpa and Old Raven Man, two old men. She actually thought she smelled licorice throat drops on Grandpa's breath. As she told Lonny her dreams, she heard the swish, shuffle, swish of Old Raven Man's moccasins. He'd never worn moccasins in her dreams. Just now, was that a flash of blue beading? His soft damp-skinned cheek laid against hers?

She closed her eyes. Behind her lids she watched as Grandpa moved in front of Lonny. Gazed long and tenderly into his eyes. Placed a silvery hand, like a blessing, over his heart.

Then the old men came together again, joining arms, dancing around them, around Medicine Bluff, rhythmically nodding their heads. Dancing, old bony shoulders touching. Dancing through the hot dusty grass with a swish, shuffle, swish.

She could feel all around her, for the briefest of moments, a vast moving blanket tossing stars out into the cosmos. And a little part of her was flying out, too, like it wasn't even her. Looking down, watching carefully, it was saying: So this is the one. This is the person Grandpa told me about. But how can he have buffalo medicine? she thought with this part of her mind. He is just as lonely and crazy and screwed up as me.

12

With a fierce and inescapable light, his own ghosts hovered in front of his imagination. He closed his eyes and instantly and vividly saw open mouths. Saw vapors solidify, like black storm clouds, and then take shape. The woman sat on the ground. Held the dead child in her arms. Wailing and sobbing, she buried her face in its limp body. Sticky dark blood came from the back of its lolling head, soaking into the sleeve of her pale leather dress. And all around them, chaos. Dust and shouting and horses and people dying.

Terrified, he opened his eyes. "Let's go, okay?"

"Why?" she said. "What's wrong? Did I say something . . . ?"

He struggled to his feet and looked at her, real and beautiful, a flesh-and-blood girl in the gathering morning light; and then he opened his mouth and said, "Alexandra, I've been keeping something that belongs to you. It's something that I have to give you. Out of respect, you see. Because it's yours."

13

*H*e hurried her down the hill. But when they got to the bottom, he slowly opened the passenger's door of the truck, and then put his hand lightly on the small of her back.

"Okay?" he said. "Just sit inside. This will only take a minute."

Then, sitting in the truck cab, with the windows rolled down and the sweet wind rolling in, he reached across her knees and opened the glove compartment and pulled something out. He sat back against the seat for a minute, face tense, eyes blinking, and then he turned to her.

"I've had it a long time," he said. "It's from your dad."

She looked down at the letter he offered. She pushed the hair out of her eyes. An ordinary envelope. Her name scrawled on it with a cheap and leaky blue ballpoint. Her father's undeniable hand. It shook her up to see it. Something from him.

"But how did you get this?" she said, turning to him. "Where did it come from?"

"I was supposed to mail it. He died about two weeks after he wrote it."

She frowned at him. Her mouth went suddenly dry. She felt her whole body begin to tremble.

"How could I turn around and send you a letter from a dead man? And then I couldn't throw it out either. I've just held on to it all this time. He said it was for your birthday."

"And you didn't send it?"

Eyelids lowered, he leaned against the door, running his thumb along the chrome handle.

Astonishing. A fat letter. Nothing he'd ever written had been long. The letter that talked about the roses had been the longest. Contained the most words. And now here was Earl—her father, the shadow—grazing across her life with another letter. For her seventeenth birthday.

She tried to get it open. Her hands shook too badly. She could feel Lonny looking at her, then abruptly away, out the truck window.

He said, at last, still looking out, "Do you want me to leave?"

"Yes," she said. "I do."

"I'm sorry." His hand was opening the door. "I don't know what else to say. I'm very, very sorry." And then he got out and left her alone.

She waited until he had disappeared around the side of the cabin before she opened the envelope and carefully withdrew its contents. Unfolded the letter. Something fluttered into her lap. She picked it up. The hot wind lightly buffeted the truck. She looked down at a photograph. And into the face of her father.

14

Lonny sank down behind the cabin. Leaned back against the wood wall. Looked out over the lake. Closed his eyes and let the hot reedy-smelling wind press against him. Felt his limbs go heavy.

Now he wished he had sent the letter. He wished with all his heart he could go back to that day when Earl had drunkenly entrusted it to him. He wished he had gotten into the truck, right then, and driven over the snowy roads to town. He wished it for her, and most of all he wished it for himself.

But wishing won't change things, he thought. It's just a trick you play on yourself when you come up against something that makes you wake up inside your life.

Shit, why is this happening to me? He looked helplessly around. There was no refuge. No refuge from ghosts or memories that crowded around him. No refuge from this tenderness, for her, that shook him and seized his heart.

15

When had the picture been taken? In it, her father was gray and skinny and weather-beaten. He wore one of those snap-button plaid shirts. And a wide belt with a thick Western buckle. He looked normal. Just kind of like a worn-out cowboy. No trace of madness in his eyes, no trace at all. He wasn't smiling. He stared into the camera as if somebody had said, "Cheese," and he'd been thinking, "Screw you." From the look of him, that was probably something he thought a lot.

There were many handwritten pages, seven in all, the words cramped up like patient lines of marching ants.

Dear Alexandra Marie, So this is your seventeenth birthday. I never made it to any of your other birthdays, so I guess I'm a fool for thinking I might have made it to this one.

Pardon me for being so frank. As they say, it's the liquor talking. I guess it's good for something. Liquor has been my way of life for so many years, I hardly know what to say to people when I'm sober.

I've sure come to a different point in my life. It's like I'm passing over into something different, and I don't know exactly what it is yet. I feel as strange and restless as a sick old wolf. Like I need to hurry up and get my life in order.

So, my baby girl, you'll be a grown-up young woman by now. This means I am finally free to be frank. Just before you were born, your mother had said to me, "Earl, if you can't handle the responsibility now, then when are you ever going to?" And I guess I figured she was right. She always did stand her ground like an angel with a mission, and I always admired her for that. I decided after a particularly bad drinking binge that I had to leave town.

An alcoholic, she thought, with relief. My God, he wasn't a madman—he was just a drunk! She sank farther down in the seat of the LaFrenières' truck and continued reading:

Maybe I was too ashamed and scared to see you again. And, in all honesty, maybe I knew in my own sorry heart that I would never have been able to give your young life anything but broken promises. Life is full of maybes, Alexandra, and it doesn't always offer up second chances. And that is the sad truth.

I bet you always wondered about your old man. Why I ran off on your beautiful mother like that. Truth is, Alexandra, after her, I never wanted to marry anybody else.

Never be too scared or too proud to tell somebody you love them.

I spent a lot of years running around being a cowboy. Went to every big-city and small-town rodeo from Alberta to Saskatchewan to Manitoba and down through the midwestern United States. Won a lot of prizes, played a lot of poker, chased a lot of women, drank a lot of bourbon and rye whiskey. I took pride in being an "outlaw," as the song says. But then I stopped winning prizes. I started working on ranches, where I played a lot more poker, drank a lot more whiskey, and found one woman, in particular, who seemed to want to put up with me. Until she got sicker of me than I was of myself.

And here's the deal. Here's what happened that changed my life. When I was working on a ranch near Lethbridge, I went into town one day and bought a lottery ticket. It came through for me. The night of the day I found out I'd won, I went out, dead sober, under the stars. I was naked except for a pair of shorts and my boots and a blanket. I went up to the top of a hill that used to be a vision-quest place for the Plains Indians. I sat up there like an old-time Indian. Wrapped up in my blanket. I sat there without food or water all night and all the next day and then for three more nights and days until the sun went down again.

During that time I prayed to the Almighty to help make me sober and change my life around. To help me see a way to make good this second chance and not to just piss it all away again, pardon my French. I was hungry and cold and lonelier than a lonely man could ever be. Around the morning of the third day—I'd lost all track of time except for the stick scratchings I made in the dirt—I figured I couldn't keep it up much longer. But I did.

A very queer thing happened while I was up there. On the third night I started seeing things. I'd done some reading on the subject, and so I knew what I was seeing was based on actual history. I saw Indian people dressed in ghost shirts. They were ghost dancing all around me. I was in the middle of it. I was scared as hell but excited, too.

Here's a bit of information for you. Call it my measly contribution to your education. Anyway, did you know, Alexandra, that in 1890, before the Battle of Wounded Knee, the Indians had a prophet? A Paiute man by the name of Wovoka. Well, Wovoka had a vision. He told the people that if they danced to call up the spirits of their ancestors and the buffalo, their former life would be restored to them just as it was before the white man came. In fact, they believed the dance would make the white man disappear altogether.

Well, in the middle of the night, in the middle of my waking dream, or whatever it was (I swear I was dead sober), I got up, a white man, and I started dancing with them. I never felt such joy before or since. And after it was over, and they all danced away in the morning mist, I watched the sun rise up over the horizon. And I felt like I was changed forever. Like I wasn't who I was before.

I laughed out loud up on that lonely hill. What a terrific, terrifying, wonderful thing. They'd got rid of one more white man by giving me the vision of an Indian. What a magnificent way to make their wish come true.

I'm not going to lie to you and tell you that I reformed and started on a life of sobriety. But I did become a more clear-eyed drunk. I became a drunk with a vision. It was that vision that led me to buying up land and building a cabin on it and writing a will. I don't want you ending up like your old man, always with your head in the clouds, never firmly planted in anything.

I think that you would like this place I bought. I chose it a year before its former owner would actually sell it to me. If I don't make it through this winter, will you tell him that we are all guardians of the land on this sacred planet? I never had the nerve to say such a thing to him in person. But I expect you are your mother's daughter, with enough spine to tell anybody anything real that they need to hear.

So I guess I'll close. Like I said last time I wrote, always look the world straight in the eye. And I might also add, don't take no crap from nobody. But if you're anything like your mother, you probably don't anyway.

Wishing you all the best in the world, my girl. And sending you, probably too late, all of my love. From your father, Earl McKay.

All of her life as she had known it just seemed to stop. All of his attention and all of his love directed at her—she could hardly believe it. She thought about her father up on that Alberta hill, dancing on the land with the spirits like it was a normal and perfectly healthy thing to do. Thought about his rapture. About the moment when his life turned. Thought with chilling ecstasy about Grandpa and Old Raven Man, dancing in her own vision, up on Medicine Bluff.

And to think that she had almost missed getting this, the most important letter of all.

16

$\mathcal{H}$e watched her walk, in a terrible calm way, around the side of the cabin and come toward him. She held out Earl's letter like a piece of evidence. And then she started in: "I can't believe you did this. I can't believe you didn't send this letter to me. This was my father. He wrote it, and he wanted me to have it. I don't care that he died, or if I was just some stranger you thought you didn't have to do anything about. What did you think you were doing all this time, keeping something so important from me? I might have seen him if I'd gotten it in time. I might have been able, at least, to be with him when he died.

"I want you to read it," she went on coldly, handing it over to him. "I want you to read every damn word. And then I want you to go away. I want you to get in your truck and get the hell away from me."

She turned her back on him and walked away. Walked imperiously around to the side. Walked like goddamn royalty up the cabin steps and slammed the door.

With a sickened heart, he began Earl's letter, forcing himself to read it with more attention than he'd given anything he'd read in a long time. And as he read, he realized that nobody knew Earl. Nobody ever had. He was at the end of his life when he wrote this letter. And he'd wanted at least his daughter to understand him. And to forgive him.

He quietly walked around the side of the cabin, went into the kitchen. He could see through to the living room, could see her perfect feet sticking out over the end of the sofa. He walked in. Her hair peeked, turtlelike, up over the collar of a weathered brown leather jacket that he recognized. Earl had worn that jacket.

"Alexandra," he said softly, putting down the letter on the little table beside the sofa. He wanted to tell her the rest of his story. He wanted her to know that he had had those same kinds of dreams, too, just like her, dogging his ass, haunting his days, bringing him to his knees.

She came out from inside her father's jacket. She unzipped it and opened her dark eyes and looked unwaveringly up at him. Then she pulled the fur collar up to her cheeks and closed her eyes again. Closed them tight.

He could tell that she was praying to see her father. He knew her. He knew how she would lie there, stretched out, a ball of tension slowly rising up her body. How she would be pressed by ghosts and dreams and the weight of her own incomprehensible longing. And that she would wait for whatever time it took. Wait for Earl McKay to materialize in the white sunlight that was spiraling through the window onto her eyelids.

He tore along the road. The LaFrenière land, the land that he could hardly remember not knowing, was now a speck no bigger than a fly's eye in the blue of heaven.

He jammed on the brakes, then pumped them. The truck slid dangerously, back end grinding over the gravel, and came to a halt. He got out. Slammed the door. Walked down the road. Felt trapped under the prairie sky. Grabbed up a handful of gravel. Hurled it at the horizon. Ran and yelled until his lungs burned to almost bursting. Then he stopped, bending over the road, gasping for breath, and turned around.

Back near the truck, he sank down at the side of the road, sitting in a tight ball, arms locked around his knees, staring into the ditch. Until he heard another vehicle coming along. Saw it trailing dust down the road. He quickly leaped up, dusting off his jeans. Walked nonchalantly back to the truck.

The driver slowed, just as he'd thought he would. You couldn't ever do anything on these roads without someone coming along, asking if you needed help, about how Pop was, wanting to discuss their crops, their kids, their wives, bingo night at the Legion Hall in town, the latest doings of some neighbor.

He gave a small firm country wave. Kicked at a tire like he was testing it. Got back in the truck and lurched away before he had to stop and talk.

* * *

"Thought you were supposed to be at work today," said Pop when he got back. "Too busy chasing that little girl around Earl's place, I guess."

Earl's place. The blood pulsed in his ears. He went and got the ax out of the shed and started chopping wood. Each log that split cleanly down the middle was one log further away from her. Away from the ghosts. Away from everything.

Pop sat down to watch him. Wood chips blasted everywhere. Lonny didn't stop until he'd counted up twenty-nine split logs.

"Working up quite a sweat," Pop observed mildly. "What demon's got at your back today, son?"

"None," said Lonny, throwing another log onto the growing heap.

"Something's lit your tail, that's for sure. Wouldn't have anything to do with Earl's daughter, would it?" he pressed. "I wish you good luck with her, son. I wouldn't be saying this to you but for the fact that there's something about her that's real special." Pop got up then, pushed around a few wood chips with his toe, and wandered off.

Lonny heaved another log onto the block, took a deep breath, and swung the ax again. He was fed up with dead people. He wanted to live his life and fall in love and be a good person instead of always feeling like shit. Like nothing would ever be right.

17

*W*hen she couldn't see him behind her closed eyes, when finally all she sensed in the sunny room were her own heartbeats rising up and out of her body like invisible birds, she sat up to read his letter again. She perched his photograph against the green stone candleholder and then from time to time lifted her eyes from his words to look at his flat image. She tried to imagine him younger. Maybe his hair had once been the same color as hers. But the picture showed a washed-out grizzled quality, a kind of undefinable yellowish gray. She tried to connect with the eyes, the angry look, of this father who was sending her "probably too late, all of my love."

She lay back and shut her eyes again. And then something touched her shoulder. It was the steadying memory of Grandpa's warm hand. And once again, she was nine years old.

They would be out on Spirit Lake in the boat all day long so that, coming back onto solid land, she could still feel the watery rocking motion. Grandpa would follow her, weaving on her feet, as they walked up the path to their tent. Always, at some point, his hand would come to rest on her shoulder.

At night, as they bedded down, and she closed her eyes, their tent became a boat, rocking, rocking, rocking on the water. "Breathe deep," Grandpa would say in the darkness. He'd open the tent flap to the dazzling Milky Way. "Look! Those are the ancestors up there. Maybe you can even see your grandmother's face in one of those beautiful stars."

She'd look up into the vast cosmos, which also made her dizzy. But in the end it was the stars that balanced the rocking motion. A few hours later she'd wake up feeling calm, and the tent flap would be closed, and Grandpa would be snoring, and she would snuggle, like a cozy worm, close to the earth in her sleeping bag.

Alex sat up and looked at the brown sleeves of her father's jacket, looked at her own hands emerging from the cuffs. He had once been inside this jacket. She tried to feel his memory. Instantly, she felt sick.

I decided after a particularly bad drinking binge that I had to leave town. . . . I'm not going to lie to you and tell you that I reformed and started on a life of sobriety. . . .

The cabin walls undulated with the shadows of trees. She stood up and lurched across the living-room floor. Opening the front door, she eased down into the long grasses. For a moment she thought that she might throw up. She wondered how often he had felt that way. How many years had he been an alcoholic? She stood and wobbled toward the lake shore.

But, once again, she felt the steadying pressure of Grandpa's hand on her shoulder. She stopped and looked up, breathing deeply, pulling blue sky like a vapor into her body. Then, more balanced and sure-footed, she turned south on the land.

Her cotton socks poking up out of brown boots with red laces. Red willow branches slapping past her arms. Her pale jeans with the frayed cuffs. The bluish green lichen on black oak trunks.

After a short distance, in a clearing, she crouched low to the earth. She watched the way the sun filtered through the white poplars past her shoulder. She watched the way all the little green plants poked up and through every dead thing. The way the wet ground glistened where a little trickle of golden water came seeping up through it, then went sliding down past the trees to the lake. She watched a small frog with yellow eyes sit in a sleepy froggy daydream not more than a foot away. She slowly reached out her hand and eased a finger under one silky cool frog toe and thought that this was true magic. They could have been shaking hands, and all it did was blink.

She was now aware of the squeaking poetry of her father's leather jacket, of how it must have sounded to his own ears, of how he must have felt on good days.

I think that you would like this place I bought. . . .

And then she heard what she thought he might have wanted her to hear. First came the buzzing of one wild bee, then the sweet whisper of leaves. A cow lowed very far away. The hum of crickets, the drumming beak of the woodpecker, the sucking sound of heels in mossy mud. Sound of lapping waves on stone, sound of beetle legs on crispy leaf, sound of blood pulsing in ear, sound past silence, sound past sunlight, smell past sunlight, taste past sunlight, taste of ecstasy.

18

*D*eena sat across from him, in a booth at the back
of the deli, her blue eyes smudged with mascara and
fatigue. She squinted through the smoke she inhaled
from her cigarette.

"I know," she said. "I know, I know, I have to
quit."

She stabbed out the glowing end in the tin ashtray
and pushed it over beside the ketchup and the napkin
dispenser. "When your mom was alive, I thought
about quitting even before she did. After she died, I
abused tobacco even more. Now, that's stupid, isn't
it." She reached across the booth and took his hand.
"You didn't just come in here for a burger. You
haven't touched it."

He didn't know where to begin. Didn't know how
to cut through the years of not speaking his mind. He
looked at her fingers curled tightly with his. Remembered Tammy's hands and Jen's hands and his own
carelessness with them and the land and the people
he most loved.

"Deena," he said, pulling away, "what do you do when you feel so lonely even your teeth ache?"

"I don't know, sweetie. You are asking the queen of loneliness."

"How come. You and Pop. Never. You know."

"Oh, that." She blushed right up past her freckled neck and into her wiry blond hairline. "I thought there was a spark . . . you know . . . that was after, *after* your mom died. But he was too cut up, and I guess I was too set in my ways."

She let those half-truths hang around in the air for a while. He watched as she lit up another cigarette.

"I love you, Deena," he said softly, feeling his heart crumble in a million pieces in front of her. "I always have, and I just thought I should tell you that. You know, I sometimes think we don't tell people stuff. Until it's too late."

Deena spoke right into his face. "Tell me what's resting so heavy inside you. You have to say it out loud, Lonny."

He picked up the pepper shaker, rolled it between his hands, set it carefully down on the table again. He remembered his mother's hair, the way it rested around her in the coffin. The way her face hadn't looked like her face, the way her hands, the delicate bones in each finger, looked like somebody else's hands, the way he felt, as if he were swimming in grief, seeing her eyes closed, the lashes resting against her cheeks, and Pop's warm arm around him, leading him away, and the priest in his robes with his brown shoes that had mud on one toe.

"You've never wanted to talk to me about her," Deena said, reading his mind. "You've always had these walls around you. I felt like I shouldn't pry. Maybe I was scared to. Scared of what I might find. Everybody's a coward, you know. We all just have different things that keep us awake at night."

Lonny's heart lurched. "I'm doing the best I can. I don't know how else to do what I've been doing. I don't know where else to turn. That's why I came in here tonight. You know that property of ours that got bought up? Well, the girl who owns it now is out there, on the land, and she's mad as hell at me. And I'm scared to have her be there by herself. I just know that something bad is going to happen to her."

"Something bad?" Deena sucked on her cigarette, stabbed it out, breaking it in two, peered fiercely at him.

He blurted out, "It's my fault that Mom died."

"Lonny," she said carefully, leaning forward, "little kids make up all kinds of dumb stuff in their heads. They think that they're magicians. Like just by closing their eyes and wishing stuff, they can make terrible things happen. But you know that isn't true. You're all grown up now. You know there is no such thing as terrible magic."

"Could have fooled me," he said, shivering. "Goddammit, I'm cold. Deena. You've got the air-conditioning turned way up in this place again."

"Stay right where you are. Don't you move."

It was eleven o'clock at night. Deena got up and hurried out her last customer, old Donald Finnbogason, always the first one there in the morning and the last one to leave. Then she stuck her head in the back and told everybody to go home, that she'd wash up, finish up, do the cash. After that she locked the front door. Moved the red-and-black cardboard sign in the window from OPEN to CLOSED. She came back with a piece of pumpkin pie with whipped cream and a cup of hot black coffee, set these in front of Lonny, picked up his cold untouched burger plate and sent it sliding down the opposite counter.

She sat down across from him again. "Lonny, if I ever loved a kid, it's you. And I think that I have failed you badly. And that's why we are going to sit here, right into next week if we have to. You have my total and undivided attention."

He could see his mother now as if she were standing right beside them. The pink sweater she often wore. Her fingernails perfect elongated moons. The way her feet slid along the floor when she was tired. The matter-of-fact way she went about doing everything. And when she was angry, a small gesture—a magazine sliding onto the floor, an icy shake of the head, a word, a look—everything about the way she moved, a slow economy of efficient energy. So many things about her that he had forgotten began to rush back.

"Start talking," said Deena, "and don't leave out a thing."

19

At five o'clock in the morning, the red dawn rose beyond the big east-facing windows of Deena's Deli. His mother's spirit had eased herself in beside Deena, and Lonny knew that he was seeing things again. Her face was turned so that he could clearly see the way her fine black hair always escaped and fell across her ear no matter how many times she tried to clip it back.

Deena looked across at him and said, "We need to pack it up here. I can't keep awake much longer. You didn't even eat your pie. So"—she gave Lonny a wan smile—"you're going to set your heart at ease finally and go and talk to him."

He got up out of the booth, went around, and pulled her, dog tired, up out of her seat. She leaned against him, and he clung to her, trembling.

"It'll be okay," she said, stroking his back. "Go on now."

"Deena," he whispered in her ear, "I know Mom wouldn't want you to give up on Pop."

And then he was in the truck, driving away, one hand on the steering wheel, the other, for courage, on the cracked red vinyl seat, the very edge of it, where, drawn in ballpoint ink by himself one day when he was fourteen and bored and missing Mom, was a tiny blue heart pierced with an arrow.

"I'm going to put the coffee on, Pop," he said when he got home. "I've got something I have to tell you."

Pop rolled over in his bed and rubbed his eyes. "You were out again all night," he said. "I wish you'd give a fellow some warning. So I wouldn't always have to be lying here in the middle of the night, worrying about you."

"Please," said Lonny, "come on out to the kitchen. Get up now, because I really need you to do that."

He made coffee, and Pop came and sat down, and then Lonny told him everything. And when it was all finished, when everything was finally all out in the open, Pop sat there stunned, leaning forward, and said, "All this time . . . ?"

Lonny didn't trust himself to answer. He nodded his head and stared at Pop and couldn't take his eyes away. It was like looking at hope coming up over the horizon.

"I thought . . . the LaFrenière land . . . *That's* why you didn't want it?"

Lonny nodded again and felt a gasp shake his body.

Pop dropped his head, wiped his eyes. "I was so busy with my own grief."

"I'm *so* sorry, Pop."

Pop raised his eyes. "Why couldn't you have told me?"

"She said it would kill you."

"Who said that? Your mother?"

"She died feeling disappointed in me."

"My God," said Pop.

He got up quickly and came to Lonny and wrapped his arms around him just like a big sheltering tree. "There, there," he said as Lonny wept and clung to him. "There, there," he said, awkwardly kissing the top of Lonny's head. "You don't have to keep suffering, son. It's over now. I forgive you."

Lonny nodded, pulled away, choked back his sobs. But more tears kept coming. Finally, he threw back his head in his chair and wept uncontrollably.

Pop kept on talking, whether out of relief or concern, Lonny wasn't sure, but his words rippled along like rain. And then Lonny stopped crying, and for the first time since he could remember, he felt calm.

"The year before I met your mother," Pop was saying, "I went over Dinlaren way. There's an elder over there by the name of Joe Dakotah, and he runs a sweat lodge. Anyway, I went there to be purified and find some meaning to my life, and right in the middle of all that praying and chanting, I get the idea for that newspaper ad, looking for a companion. And, by gum, didn't it work out pretty good, too. I found you and my Margaret. A little prayer sitting right next to Mother Earth never hurts when you have a troubled heart. Would you like me to arrange for you to meet Joe?"

"I already have," said Lonny, wiping his eyes. "Two nights ago. He was over at Robert's, talking to Daryl. He's a scary guy. He makes you see the truth."

"That's good then. Very, very good." Pop slowly nodded his shaggy bear head.

Lonny hung his own head, looked at his hands, raised them, and covered his eyes. He was so tired, bone weary. Light gathered like kinks of electricity. A buffalo walked across his vision. Left to right. Disappeared. Walked around behind his head and slowly began to cross again.

"Will you do me a favor?" said Pop.

Lonny opened his eyes. "Anything, Pop."

"It's about Earl. I figured his daughter should have the choice of doing what she wants with her father's ashes."

"You've kept them all this time?"

"Was I wrong to do that?" said Pop.

"No. I guess you did whatever you thought you should do."

"He wanted the cheap urn. A little white cardboard box. I worried about that. What the family might think. 'But anything extra,' he told me a couple of days before he died, 'anything extra off this old buffalo is fat that I want my daughter to have.' So I said, 'Okay, Earl, the cheap urn it is.'"

Lonny shook his head and smiled.

"And then he says, 'Ever see human ashes?' 'Well,

no, I haven't,' I tell him. 'They're heavy,' he says. 'Got little pieces of bone and teeth in them. So make sure they pretty them up, okay?' 'What exactly do you mean?' I say. 'Well,' says Earl, 'you know, she'll just look at them and get real turned off. People,' he says, 'have this idea of *spreading them*. Know what I mean? So, Tom,' he says, looking at me with his eyes, and they're all burning up with pneumonia, 'we have to be practical, okay? For her sake? So could you ask them, please, to put them in a grinder?' "

"You did that?"

"It was a dying man's wish. You can say what you want about Earl, but when he was sober, he did have this very down-to-earth personal side." Hands on his knees, levering himself out of his chair, he said, "They're out in the shed. I'll go get them. I think you should be the one to give them to her. You need to go back and make your peace with her and the land."

"Pop, she doesn't even want to talk to me."

"We'll see about that. Go and clean yourself up now. You look like you've been sleeping in a swamp."

Twenty minutes later, opening the truck door, Pop set the little white cardboard box on the seat beside Lonny. "Well, Earl," he said, addressing the box, "looks like you're finally going to meet your daughter."

He closed the door, leaned into the open window. "You're going to be okay," he said, this time to Lonny. He pulled back and slapped the side of the truck.

Lonny drove away, stealing glances in the rearview

mirror. Pop raising his hand, waving. Pop dropping his hand, lowering his head, lost in a private moment. Pop looking at the sky. And as he slowly turned, then walked back toward the empty house, Lonny understood that Pop would be okay, too.

20

She gave up, disappointed, and put down the phone. She opened the refrigerator, pulled out a box of orange juice, a bag of bagels, a tub of cream cheese. She had wanted to tell her mother about how she'd come back from the clearing, dazzled, cleaned out in her spirit. How she then lay on the sofa with all the windows and doors open and her head so filled with sounds, growing sounds, frogs everywhere. "He's here! And here! And here!" they sang as they leaped in light. Leaped in shade. Trilled from trees. From under rocks. From up on top of the mound.

She'd intended, later, to go out naked under the stars, just as he had done, with only her quilt wrapped around her. And she would have stayed out all night, too. But she fell asleep right there, in the fullness of day, in this cabin, on this land that had somehow become saturated with her father's life. She didn't dream except for the clear green froggy light that glowed, then gradually dimmed, behind her closed eyes.

And then she slept through the night. She knew that as she slept the moon had changed position in the sky. And the stars, flung across the vast prairie cathedral, beamed their steady memory of light. They were all up there now, her grandmother and Grandpa and her dad, every one of them taking their place with the ancestors.

She went out to eat breakfast on the steps outside the kitchen. Under the early morning sun, she flipped off the cream-cheese lid. The moan of the LaFrenières' truck sounded at the top of the road. Grew closer. Her heart began to pound high in her throat as Lonny pulled onto the land. By the time he got out of the truck, her mouth had gone dry. Her top lip stuck to her teeth. Her legs were weak.

Lonny stopped and stood silently in the grass. She folded her arms and felt his eyes looking at her.

"It seems," he said, "I'm always bringing you things that are really tough to give. And are even tougher to receive."

She raised her eyes. He walked toward her. Nestled in his palms was a small white box. He climbed up the little steps and sat down beside her.

"What's this?"

"Your dad's ashes."

"Oh," she said, and then felt as if she were plunging headlong into deep dark water.

He set the box down. "Pop figured that you'd know what you wanted to do with them. He wanted me to bring them to you."

He sat quietly, perched at the edge of the step. Looking at his feet. Glancing at hers. Waiting.

And then he started talking quietly. "Your dad had been drinking pretty steady since Christmas, and he was drunk when he got to our house. He'd walked all that way, in a blizzard, just so we'd get that letter and mail it for him. But even if I'd mailed it right away, I don't know if you'd have met him in time. He got sick right after that. He was in the hospital five days later. He never came out again."

She looked down at the lake. This was a view her father would have looked at again and again in the short time he was here. Did it bring him comfort? Everything was so complicated in this life. It's just like Grandpa had always said, always the good and the bad together.

"Let's go somewhere else," Lonny said finally. "Let's go down to the lake. It's nice there. You can see little minnows swimming. The water is full of life this time of year."

She walked ahead. A big gray rock edged the shoreline. There was room for two or more, and she sat down and Lonny sat near her. They stared out at the water. The sun warmed her shoulders. She ran her fingers along the sun-heated rock, and she could feel the warmth of his body close by.

"I didn't know who to be mad at," she finally said. "Life is so unfair sometimes." She turned to him. "It's a wonderful letter. I'm glad you kept it. I'm glad you didn't throw it out."

"I should have sent it," he said quickly. "I know that now."

Do something, she thought. Or was it her thought? In a few minutes he'll drive away, said this thought, and you'll be alone again. With your father's ashes.

All it takes is moving one inch. That's what makes the difference. Moving your hand just a bit. Making your little finger lift ever so gently toward his. Contact, like lightning bugs.

And suddenly she is in his arms, her mouth against his neck, his sweet hair a curtain around them. His lips, his tongue. Wind blowing off the lake. His beating heart.

21

$\mathcal{H}$e felt as if he'd just jumped off a cliff and didn't know or care where or when he'd hit bottom. He held his fall for a quarter of a century. The world spun many times. This is what it's like to free-fall into somebody's heart, he thought. Maybe I'll die.

She was the first to start breathing again. He held her forehead against his, mentally counted to four, then pulled away.

She had that look that girls get. Even the smartest girls. Like their brains have just left their bodies and won't be returning anytime real soon. Usually this was a great sign. Today it finally made him want to put on the brakes. Then her vision seemed to clear. He watched her soft look harden into little points of dark darting flame.

"Relax," he said, feeling shaky and full of crazy love.

"Boy," she said, her eyes tearing up. She looked out at the lake. "Boy, oh, boy."

He watched big fat tears flow down her face. Looked

away. Felt the way he had that first day when Pop took him up to the top of Medicine Bluff. Felt that joy again. Felt that pulse of rapture go racing like fire along his skin.

"I've never met anybody quite like you," he said, looking at her sidelong, sliding his eyes away again.

"Damn right, and don't you forget it," she said, swiping at her tears with trembling fingers.

"You make me shaky." He laughed nervously.

"Is this good or bad?"

He sat there, caught by the wonder of her, imagined her back in a school playground somewhere, hanging upside down from a swing by her scabby knees. Inside her, he thought, is that little person still. And I have to be careful with her. I have to be very, very careful.

22

*G*radually, as his story unraveled, as he told it to her, his eyes soft and clear, she understood everything. This is my place now, she was thinking, but he still loves it.

The ghosts of memory swirled around them. And then another story began to unravel. "One winter," she told him, "I found a sparrow in the snow. It must have flown against the window. Its beak was bleeding, and it had managed to dig itself into a snowbank, and I think maybe it was slowly freezing to death."

Lonny gazed into the green glinting water. I don't know him, but I do, she thought. Everything until now, in our lives, has been leading to this moment. She moved closer to him again. Hip to hip, knee to knee. I don't care about what I should do or shouldn't do, she thought. This feels right. I like him. And it's good to feel this fire in my body and to comfort him and to be here with him by this lake.

"I pulled the bird out of the snowbank," she continued. "I took it into the house and wrapped it in a towel and phoned Grandpa, and he brought over an old birdcage he had at his place. He looked at the sparrow and said, 'It just needs rest, that's all.' And then he eased it into the cage."

Lonny sat up a little straighter. He lifted his hand and placed his fingers gently on the bone at the back of her neck. Then she sighed and put her head on his chest, and his arm came slowly around her, like a question.

"Well," said Alex, "we left that sparrow in a dark room, and in a couple of hours it started hopping around the cage. I gave it some chopped-up pecans, and it ate those. And then it started to flutter around, clinging to the metal sides. 'It's ready to go now,' Grandpa said. But I wasn't ready yet to let it go. It was freezing outside. How would it survive?"

Lonny put his other arm around her, hugging her, tenderly stroking the flesh below her sleeve.

" 'Sparrows are tough,' Grandpa said. And then he waited, like always, for me to make up my mind. The sparrow was getting desperate. Beating its wings against the silver bars. It was awful. And I felt, I don't know, sick, I guess. Finally I put my hand in the cage and captured it. It bit me. It was strong. Its thoughts were already out there in the cold north wind. It bit me again before I could get it through the open window. And then it flew out over the snow. Grandpa said, 'Someday after I'm gone, you'll think about this day.' "

For a long time she and Lonny lingered there, by the lake. Some people, she was thinking, don't ever get to know how wonderful it is to do something so simple as this. Just sitting side by side, together, on a big sunny rock.

23

*U*nder the blue starry night he sat on Earl's steps and waited for her. There were ancient whisperings in the cosmos. The full moon shone in a beautiful way on the abandoned LaFrenière cabin, on its soft silvery wood. This is what I've learned about waiting, he thought. If you wait with all of your senses, you don't wait empty.

And then light from Earl's kitchen flooded in behind him. She came out, wrapped in a long quilt, her hair gleaming down her back like the sheen of an animal diving under water.

They walked up together. Medicine Bluff irradiated a smoky haze. Halfway up, poplar leaves clicked, old women's tongues. Near the crest of the hill, she turned. Cradled in her arms, glowing with moon, were her father's ashes.

She opened the box and set it down on the sage-smelling land. In the space of four heartbeats, her left hand came away, pale with the powder of her father's bones. She made a fist, held it high, danced in a circle, threw back her head, and howled like a wolf.

He watched as she released Earl McKay's ashes. Some scattered down the hill. The rest flew like a blessing over a large scar of dark green and were carried away on the strong night winds.

acknowledgments

This book owes its being to many rich sources, not the least of which is the spirit of the land that whispered to me all through my lucky freewheeling childhood in nature.

A huge debt of gratitude is due the First Nations people as a whole, those female and male voices who speak their passionate worldwide warrior truth.

There are, as well, certain individuals I wish to thank for their loving and generous participation in the journey: Brian Brooks, Maureen Hunter, Margaret Shaw-MacKinnon, Jean Kari, Judy V. Wilson, Dominic Barth, Patsy Aldana, Shelley Tanaka, Melanie Kroupa, Mary Kate McDonald, Laara Fitznor, Virginia Maracle, Sidura Ludwig, Beth Burrows, Todd Schaus, Brock Adams, Sonny Clarke, Gary Granzberg, Della Dewart, George Toles, Alice Drader, Pauline Wood Steiman, Mona Lynne Howden, David Stewart, and my friends at Red Willow Lodge—Jules and Margaret Lavallee, Betty Rodway, and Gerry Scharien—*migwitch*, you guys. I'll always remember that the mosquitoes leave at exactly 11:26 at night.

The Manitoba Arts Council and the Canada Council, always there for artists in this country, once again came through with greatly appreciated and generous funding.

Last, and most humbly, I want to honor the spirits of the ancestors who guided my waking visions and nighttime dreams and never once gave up on this willing but frequently dense translator.